THE WINTER OF THE ROBOTS

Also by Kurtis Scaletta

Mudville

A *Booklist* Top 10 Sports Book for Youth

"*Mudville* will hit a home run with baseball fans of all ages."
—*Sports Illustrated Kids*

"Scaletta's debut is a gift from the baseball gods." —*Booklist*

"[Scaletta] balances perceptive explorations of personal and domestic issues perfectly with fine baseball talk and . . . absorbing play-by-play."
—*School Library Journal*

Mamba Point

"Entertaining and touching." —*The New York Times Book Review*

★ "Scaletta's expertly voiced narrative offers an experience of Africa . . . in a tale tinted with magical realism that is by turns scary and very funny."
—*Kirkus Reviews*, Starred

"Funny, adventuresome, and at times serious, the story is about a boy trying to figure out who he is and where he belongs." —*The Washington Post*

"Suspenseful, strange and enthralling." —*The Buffalo News*

The Tanglewood Terror

Winner of the Minnesota Readers' Choice Award

A Kids' Indie Next List Selection

"This book is nonstop action. Scaletta is great at making the bizarre and possibly supernatural seem, if not ordinary, completely plausible."
—Minneapolis *Star Tribune*

"Scaletta imbues something utterly ordinary . . . with a sort of mysticism. . . . The author's examinations of sibling dynamics are on point, and the . . . relationship between Eric and his littler brother is thoughtfully developed. . . . Plenty to like in Tanglewood." —*The Bulletin of the Center for Children's Books*

THE WINTER OF THE ROBOTS

Kurtis Scaletta

ALFRED A. KNOPF
NEW YORK

THIS IS A BORZOI BOOK PUBLISHED BY ALFRED A. KNOPF

Visit us on the Web! randomhouse.com/kids

Educators and librarians, for a variety of teaching tools, visit us at RHTeachersLibrarians.com

Library of Congress Cataloging-in-Publication Data
Scaletta, Kurtis.
The winter of the robots / Kurtis Scaletta. — 1st ed.
p. cm.
Summary: There's something lurking in the junkyard in Jim Knox's neighborhood, and it's up to him and his friends (and science-fair rivals) to put their robot-building skills together in order to defeat it.
ISBN 978-0-307-93186-3 (trade) — ISBN 978-0-375-97110-5 (lib. bdg.) —
ISBN 978-0-307-97562-1 (ebook)
[1. Robots—Fiction.] I. Title.
PZ7.S27912Wi 2013
[Fic]—dc23
2012036376

Printed in the United States of America

October 2013

10 9 8 7 6 5 4 3 2 1

First Edition

For Mom and Dad, finally

PART I

OTTERCAMS

CHAPTER 1

None of this would have happened if I hadn't picked a girl over a robot.

On the first day of school after winter break, Mr. Cole, our science teacher, hit us with a big assignment: the school science fair. We were supposed to pair up. As usual, my partner was Oliver. He'd been my best friend since we were toddlers.

"So what do you want to do, another robot?" I asked him on the bus ride home. Last year, our project was a three-foot-tall robot that steamrolled a papier-mâché diorama of Minneapolis. Oliver made the robot, and I made the diorama. The project won an honorable mention, which was good for sixth graders. Now that we were in seventh grade, Oliver wanted to win a first-place ribbon and compete at the district science fair.

"Yeah, I want to make another robot," he said. "A better robot."

The bus rumbled to a stop, and the door opened to let in a blast of icy air, but nobody got off. The bus was mostly empty. There was a home basketball game, and all of the normal kids had stayed after school to watch it. All of the normal kids, that was, except for Rochelle. She lived on my block, but I didn't know her that well. She caught me looking at her and waved. I looked back at Oliver.

"Can we do the same thing twice in a row?" I was only half interested in the conversation now. Rocky—that was what kids called her—Rocky waving at me was distracting. Girls didn't usually wave at me. I wondered what it meant, if anything. Was she saying, "Hey, caught you checking me out"? Or was she saying, "Howdy, neighbor"? Maybe it was nothing.

"We're not doing the same thing," said Oliver. It took me a moment to remember what he was talking about. "We're going to make a completely new robot."

"It's the same *idea*."

"That's what scientists do. They revise an idea, evolve it, and make it better." Both of Oliver's parents were scientists, so he would know. He was a mad scientist in training. He already had the brilliant mind, the wild hair, and the thick glasses. All he needed was a hunchbacked assistant.

The bus turned onto the bridge across the Mississippi River. The houses were smaller on our side of the river, a bit more run-down and closer together. North Minneapolis is considered the worst part of Minneapolis, but we lived in the nicest part of North, in a neighborhood called Camden.

Mom says it's the Edina of North Minneapolis. You have to be from around here to get that joke.

Rocky looked intently out the window, searching the riverbanks. If I had any courage, I would have shouted out something witty—"Lose a contact lens down there?"—but I didn't. She caught me looking at her again. This time she didn't wave, but she did smile.

"What will the robot destroy this time?" I asked Oliver. His robots always destroyed stuff. His ideal project would probably be an eight-foot-tall robot that stormed around the auditorium smashing all the other projects to smithereens.

"That's the great part," he said. "We'll pit it against last year's robot."

"You'd let Robbie get beat up?"

"It's a machine, Jim. You can't get sentimental."

"I don't see the point."

"It's more challenging. The cityscape tested the robot's mobility, but it didn't fight back. What I really like is robot battles. I would have done it last year, but I didn't have time to build two robots."

"I mean, I don't see why it has to destroy anything. Why can't it . . . fold laundry or something?"

"You sound like my mother," he said.

"I sound like a guy who has to do his own laundry." I stole another look at Rocky, but now all I could see was the back of her head.

"Battles are more theatrical," he explained. "That's all."

"What am I going to do?"

"Good question." He didn't come up with an answer before the bus stopped to let him off.

"Do you want to come over?" he asked. "We could get started."

"Nah. I have to move a snowbank before dark."

"OK. I'll email you some sketches." As the bus pulled out again, I watched him hurry down the icy sidewalk toward home, with his hands stuffed in his pockets and his knit hat not quite straight on his head.

He did have an assistant, I realized. He had me.

I didn't have a hunched back yet, but I would by the end of the winter. Dad made me do all the shoveling, and it was the snowiest winter in Minneapolis since I'd been born. There was a six-foot pile of snow by the driveway where I'd dumped all the snow so far. Now I had to move the entire mountain before it snowed again; otherwise, there would be no place to put the new stuff.

The next bus stop was right in front of my house. I dropped my backpack inside and went straight for the shovel. An hour later I was already hurting, and I'd barely made a dent. Why didn't Oliver build a robot that shoveled snow? I wondered.

"Hey," said a girl's voice behind me. I lowered the shovel and turned around. It was Rocky.

"Hey," I said. "You aren't at the game?" Like I hadn't even noticed her on the bus.

"Nah," she said. "You don't have a snowblower?" She eyed the metal storage shed sitting on our lawn next to the garage.

"Nope. That's my dad's stuff," I said. "He sells—"

"Security systems, I know. He keeps trying to talk my dad into buying one."

"Ha. Sorry about that."

"Don't be," she said. "Do you want to borrow our blower?"

"Is it cool with your dad?"

"Oh, he'd freak if he knew, but he won't be home until after midnight."

"Um . . ."

"I'm kidding!" she said. "Seriously, it's fine."

"Thanks. Seriously, that would be awesome."

"Just being neighborly," she said.

Even if I'd known she was setting me up, I would have used the snowblower.

My little sister Penny was waiting for me inside. She's in third grade.

"You cheated!" she said.

"Cheated on what?"

"You used the neighbors' snow machine."

"So what? Dad wants me to clear the driveway. He never said I had to *shovel* it."

"So you don't mind if I tell him?"

"Nope. Go right ahead."

I saw her eyes dim and then brighten.

"What if I told the *neighbor*?"

"She said I could use the blower."

"You talked to the girl. Not Mr. Battleship. It's *his* machine."

The neighbors' name was Blankenship, but Battleship would have been a good name for Rocky's dad. He was huge.

"All right. What do you want to keep your mouth shut?"

"I don't know. Something good."

"I'll watch that DVD with you, if you want," I suggested. She'd gotten one for Christmas we'd already seen a hundred times. Something about a princess and her champion horse who was really a guy who'd been turned into a horse by a witch. I sat through it twice in a row on New Year's Eve so she wouldn't tell Mom and Dad I watched a horror movie on cable.

"Nah," she said. "I'll decide later."

Penny had a hole in her heart when she was born, but they didn't discover it until she was three. She didn't have the energy toddlers were supposed to have, so a doctor ran some tests. He could tell that her heart was pumping some used-up blood back into her body before it got fresh oxygen. They did an X-ray and saw a tiny hole. Penny had to have surgery to patch it up. Mom and Dad and everybody else kept saying everything would be OK, and it turned out they were right, but it didn't feel OK at the time—not to me. I figured they were telling me that because I was an eight-year-old.

I didn't see her at the hospital until after the operation. I spent the night with Aunt Ingrid, and we went to see Penny the next day. She looked so small and scared in the kid-sized bed. She had wires and tubes coming out of her. Until then I'd been jealous of her and annoyed by her and occasionally awed by her, but that was the first time I realized I *loved* her. I knew I was supposed to, but that was the first time I felt it. She's fine now, but she gets checked up once a month to make sure her blood is getting enough oxygen and her heart is beating right. Anyway, that's why I don't mind letting her push me around. Besides, she only asks me to do stuff with her. It's not like she asks me for money. It's not like I had any to give her, if she did.

Oliver IM'd me that evening.

Oliver: I know what u can do! U can make dummy robots. New robot can battle them. Save Robbie for the district competition.

Jim: Make them out of what?

Oliver: Shoeboxes & tinfoil. I'll put a little motor in so they can run away, etc.

Jim: Why is my part always arts & crafts?

Oliver: lol

Jim: Not kidding.

Oliver: lol anyway.

Jim: ☹

Oliver: Just trying to help.

Jim: Maybe I'll come up with my own project.

Oliver: Come on.

Jim: Srsly.

Oliver: We need partners. U know that. Teams of 2.

Jim: I know. I mean w/someone else.

Oliver: Like who?

A second chat window popped up.

Rochelle: Do you have a partner for science fair?

Jim: Talking to Oliver about it now. Nothing def.

Rochelle: I have a cool idea. Want in?

Jim: Srsly? U want to be partners?

I waited for the explanation. "Rochelle is typing," the status bar told me, but nothing came up. I checked the chat with Oliver in the meantime. He'd left a series of messages.

Oliver: Who is ur partner?

Oliver: There's nobody. Admit it.

Oliver: Where are you?

Oliver: Fine, be that way.

The last message told me he was now off-line. I closed the window and went back to the chat with Rocky.

Rochelle: You have something I need.

Jim: Like what?

There was another pause. I was about to fire off a "?" when she came clean.

Rochelle: I need cams. U prolly have some.

It all made sense now. Why she lent me the snowblower. The way she eyed the storage shed.

Rochelle: Is that doable?

Jim: Maybe. What for?

Rochelle: I want to monitor urban wildlife.

Jim: Like what? Squirrels? Crows?

Rochelle: Otters. They live right here in the Miss. River. It would be super cool to study them.

I thought it over. I needed more friends in my life. Plus, I wanted to be equal partners with someone instead of taking orders from Oliver. On the other hand, there was no way Dad would let me use the cameras. On the other other hand, being seen with a girl would improve my status by about 8,000 percent. Plus, we'd hang out together. The thought made my heart pound.

Dad wouldn't give me *permission* to use the cameras, but I could borrow them for a few days and put them back. He would never know they were gone.

Jim: I'm in.

Rochelle: Terrific. It'll be fun, I promise.

CHAPTER 2

"Your science project is to look at fuzzy little animals?" said Oliver. I'd waited until lunchtime to tell him that I was swapping partners.

"What's wrong with studying animals?"

"It doesn't sound very scientific."

"We're observing animals and studying their behavior. Scientists do that, you know. Ever heard of Jane Goodall?"

"Obviously," he said, flicking the question away with his hand. "But it's not a science project unless you're trying to *prove* something."

"Says you."

"Says the rules," he said. He dug through his backpack and found the handout Mr. Cole had given us. " 'Hypothesis,' " he said, pointing at the top of the project description. "That's what you're trying to prove. It says right here: 'You should solve a problem or test a theory, not simply report information.' "

"So we'll come up with a hypothesis," I told him.

"How are you going to do it, anyway?" he asked. "Camp

on the riverbank? Wait until the otters accept you as one of their own?"

"Why are you being such a jerk about this?"

"Because now I don't have a partner," he grumbled.

"Ask someone else. They'd be happy for the easy A."

"I don't want to work with anyone else. Besides, they all have partners by now."

"There are twenty kids in the class," I reminded him. "Somebody needs a partner."

"Great. Watch me get stuck with the dumbest kid in class."

"Too late for that," I said. "I have a partner, remember?"

"Ha." He got up to leave, grabbing his tray. I grabbed my own and followed him to the garbage cans to dump the leftovers.

"So what's your hypothesis?" I asked.

"That by incorporating a gyroscopic accelerometer, the robot will have better mobility and better balance than the robot from last year. That radially swinging hammers are more effective at combat than forward-thrusting fists. That a polyurethane chassis filled with fiberglass foam can withstand more damage than a hollow metallic chassis. That—"

"That you can come up with more hypotheses than anyone else. Got it."

"It's all wrapped around a simple, central hypothesis," he said.

"That you can make a robot that will kick the butt of any other robot."

"Exactly."

Oliver didn't get stuck with the dumbest kid in class. He got stuck with the scariest: Dmitri Volkov.

Dmitri was huge, shaved his head, and wore clomping boots all year round. His family was from Russia. He must have been our age, but he seemed to be ten years older. He moved silently through the halls, a shark among guppies. There were rumors about him: that his dad was in the Russian mafia, and that Dmitri himself had been in trouble with the law. That he should have gone to reform school, but his dad had pulled strings. He was in the advanced classes and made the honor roll every quarter. That made him scarier. He was not a mere hoodlum, but a true super-villain in the making.

He only ever said two words to me—he was walking by me when I was at my locker, and stepped on my toe. "Excuse me," he'd said, but in such a flat way I still wasn't sure if he'd meant it. It was the kind of thing a bully would do, but Dmitri didn't have the reputation of being a bully. That seemed beneath him. He was into deeper and more dangerous things than pushing kids around.

When Mr. Cole asked who didn't have a partner yet, the only two hands that went up were Oliver's and Dmitri's. I'd left Oliver hanging on to a rope that turned out to be tied around the neck of a grizzly bear.

Oliver tried to lower his hand, but it was too late.

"Oliver, do you want to work with Dmitri?" Mr. Cole asked.

"I guess," he said. He wasn't going to say otherwise right in front of Dmitri.

"Dmitri?" he asked.

"I don't mind," he said evenly.

"Great," said Mr. Cole.

Oliver shot me a glance. It was a mixture of "help" and "you did this to me."

"Maybe it won't be that bad working with Dmitri," I told Oliver on the bus ride home. "He is a smart guy."

"I don't know how he's going to help, that's all," he said. "My machines are complicated."

"He's not going to make fake robots out of shoe boxes and tinfoil?"

"I don't see him doing that," said Oliver. The bus stopped, and we got off. "So where's your girlfriend?" he asked.

"I don't have one, but my science-fair partner usually takes the late bus. She has all kinds of activities."

"Oh. I thought maybe she was already living with the otters."

"Nobody's living with the otters."

"Whatever. Talk to you later. Some of us have robots to build." He hurried off without his Igor. He didn't need me anymore. He had a Frankenstein monster waiting in the wings.

Dad was on a sales call, and Mom had taken Penny to her monthly doctor visit. I hadn't completely made up my mind to borrow the cameras until that moment. It felt like fate was telling me it was OK. I went to the office and got the keys to the storage shed from the desk drawer. I also grabbed a Post-it pad and a pen.

I went out back and unlocked the shed. It was formidable, made of metal, with bars cinching it shut. I undid the lock and slid the door open, and quickly entered Penny's birth date on the flashing, beeping panel on the inside to the left of the door. It stopped flashing and beeping.

There were shelves on either side of the shed, and a tight aisle between them. Everything was neatly numbered. I didn't know how many security systems Dad installed in a week, but I knew business was slow. The holidays were behind us, and things hadn't picked up again. I could tell he hadn't been to the shed since the last snowfall, because there were no footprints.

There were eight boxes with the cameras I wanted. I took four from the back. I opened each box and removed the camera. They were about the size and shape of golf balls. I needed a code from inside the boxes, too, so I scribbled them on Post-it notes and stuck them to the cameras before I put them in my jacket pocket. I closed the empty boxes and put them back on the shelf the way I'd found them. I re-entered the code to arm the alarm and locked up the shed, then went back inside and replaced the key in the desk drawer. The whole operation took only a few minutes.

I knew how the cameras worked. I'd watched Dad do the demo. Each had a lithium battery inside it that would last a year, and a 3G card that uploaded digital video to a cloud server. The cameras worked in extreme weather and were waterproof. They came in perfectly smooth plastic cases that were easy to clean. The point was to conceal them somewhere and watch the video over the Internet. The cameras weren't the best Dad had to offer, but the 3G cards made them expensive.

I got on the computer in the office to set up an account on the camera company's website. I made sure there was a way to *deactivate* them when I was done, then entered each of the codes from the sticky notes so I could access the video from those cameras. I deleted the browser history as Mom and Penny swung open the back door. I could hear them stomping the snow off their boots, Mom scolding Penny for throwing her coat on the floor. By the time Mom called up to me, I'd stowed the cameras in my sock drawer. A few minutes later I remembered the Post-it notes. I'd left them in a sticky stack by the computer, and Dad would probably recognize them in a second. I hurried in, scooped them up, and shoved them in my pocket. I shredded them and threw them in my wastebasket. I changed my mind, dug them out, and shoved them in my backpack. I'd throw them away the next day at school.

I heard Dad's car in the driveway and realized something: we have a detached garage, so he'd pass by the storage shed on his way from the garage to the house. He might notice fresh footprints in the snow and wonder why I'd been in the shed.

I got up and peeked out the window. It was snowing briskly. All traces of my activity were gone. Dad was on the back porch, stamping the snow off his shoes.

Fate again. Fate was on my side.

A chat window popped up later when I was doing my homework.

Oliver: You must really like her.

Jim: Like who?

Oliver: I know what your science project is. Ottercams.

Jim: Ottercams?

Oliver: Don't play dumb. You must really like her.

Jim: Don't know what ur talking about. But want to come over tomorrow if it's a snow day?

Oliver: No. Working on my own proj.

Jim: w/Dm?

Oliver: Yes. We im'd. He's into the idea. Car nut. Can help build this, for real.

Oliver was letting Dmitri help him build the robot? He'd been my best friend since we were toddlers and wouldn't let me *touch* last year's robot.

Jim: So it all worked out. ☺

Oliver: Happy ending. Sniff.

Jim: Sniff.

Oliver: ttyl. Go chase otters & don't get caught.

CHAPTER 3

Penny woke me up by bouncing on the foot of the bed.

"No school! No school!" she said, or rather sang. "It's a snow day!"

"Great. So let me sleep."

"But there's *somebody* at the *door* for you." From the sing-songy way she said it, I knew it wasn't just anybody. "It's a *girl*," she added.

"The one from across the alley?" I guessed.

"Jim's got a girlfriend!" She bounded down the stairs, whooping it up. I hurriedly got dressed.

Mom was on the phone, so I decided not to bother her. I went downstairs, opened the back door, and saw a clean driveway and a clear sidewalk. Rocky was waiting for me, one hand resting on her dad's snowblower.

"Wow! Thanks!" I said. "This is huge!"

"I wanted you to be ready, so we can go look for otters. They love snow, and they'll leave fresh tracks. Let's go!"

"Right now?"

"They're more active in the morning," she said. "Come on."

"Give me two minutes."

I ran upstairs and got the cameras from my sock drawer. Penny caught me on the way back down.

"Where are you going?"

"I'm doing something for school," I told her. "I'll be back soon. Promise. Tell Mom I'm working on a school assignment." I flew out the back door before she could stop me.

Rocky had put the blower away and was waiting for me.

"You know how to use a blower," I said.

"Well, yeah. It's easy," she said. "My dad has taught me how to do everything. He says women get cheated out of learning stuff. I've changed the oil on a car. I've run an electric drill and a power saw. I even welded once."

"Cool." *I* hadn't done any of those things.

"Come on," she said. "Otters don't stand around waiting." We took the footpath that ran alongside Victory Drive. Enough people had already been by to pack down the snow. Rocky walked quickly, her hair swishing back and forth on her collar. I had to hustle to keep up.

"Hey, what's our hypothesis?" I asked her.

"That this technology can give us a better glimpse into the secret lives of otters," she said.

"OK." So she had a hypothesis. That was more than Oliver gave her credit for.

"Hey, can I ask you something?" she said, stopping. I nearly crashed into her.

"What?"

"This is totally cool with your dad, right?"

"Yeah, sure. Of course."

"I don't want you to get in trouble. I should have asked before."

"Thanks, but it's fine. My dad wants me to do well in school."

"Great." She turned back around and started walking. "At the science fair, we can tell everyone about his business, you know? That he sponsored it. So there's something in it for him. Maybe he'll get some new customers."

"Good idea." It was a good idea, but I'd have to find a way to kill it.

We took a shortcut across the park.

"I miss the trees," she said sadly.

"Me too." The park used to be full of maples, but a tornado had ripped right through the city last summer and wiped out most of them.

We crossed First Street. There was a tiny restaurant on the corner with a flashing neon sign of a kangaroo hopping along: SIDNEY'S DINER. HOME OF THE WORLD-FAMOUS POCKET BURGER! It was next door to a Laundromat.

"I think we can get to the river down this road." Rocky pointed a mitten down a sloping, slushy street with no sidewalks. I glanced at the street sign: WEST BANK ROAD. We took it, still going east, past a service station and a lumberyard and a demolition company. A man drove a small plow across the lot of Leftover Lumber, pushing snow into a hill that threatened to avalanche onto the lot of Clouts & Sons Excavation and Demolition. A hefty man stood in the doorway of the excavation place, watching. Maybe later he'd shove all the snow back on the lumberyard's lot. Maybe they went back and forth all winter, playing snow tennis.

We came to a tall wooden fence stretching in both directions.

"Drat," said Rocky. "We'll have to go back and find another way."

A narrow street went to the north, running along the wooden fence. It was blocked off by concrete pylons and hadn't been cleared all winter. "We can try this road," I suggested.

"Might as well," said Rocky.

Just past the pylons there was a street sign covered with snow. I booted the pole a couple of times and sent the snow crashing down.

"Half Street," I read aloud. "That's a funny name."

"It's parallel to First Street," Rocky explained. "They needed something lower, because the numbers go up the other way."

"I guess." We trudged through the snow, buried up to our knees. It was cold but weirdly fun. We were having an adventure. Rocky and I were officially friends now. Doing a school assignment together didn't make you friends, but having an adventure together did.

Half Street sloped down and curved east, dipping under

a railroad bridge. We emerged on the other side, in sight of the river, but were stopped by another fence—this one was chain-link topped with barbed wire. Beyond the fence were misshapen piles of snow.

Signs wired to the fence said PRIVATE PROPERTY and TRESPASSERS W— (half the sign was covered in snow).

"Look!" Rocky pointed a mitten at the fence. I looked and saw a brown blur leaping over one of the mounds of snow. "An otter!"

"Wow." It could have been a rat, but I hadn't seen it well, so I decided not to argue.

"What do we do now?" she asked.

"Heck. Go in." Maybe I liked her and maybe I didn't, but I wanted her to know I was cool and brave about stuff.

"Go in how?"

"Look over there." A massive tree limb was poking out of the snow near the fence about twenty feet away. We cleared the snow and saw that the branch had punched a hole right through the fence.

"The tornado must have done this," Rocky said sadly.

"Yeah," I agreed. I wondered how far this limb had traveled on the high winds to clear the way. Once again I had the feeling that fate was working to help me out.

Rocky pulled back a flap of the torn fence, and I crawled through. I was probably breaking the law, but I wasn't going to steal anything.

"Are you coming?" I asked her.

"Um." She looked at the tiny hole in the fence. "Sure. Of course."

I pulled the flap up and held it while she clambered through. We stood and brushed the snow off.

"What is this place?" she asked.

"I don't know. Let's take a look."

We walked around the pile the otter or rat had scooted over, which turned out to be a mix of worn lumber and red corrugated roofing tiles. Past that was an assortment of four-foot cubes covered with snow. Rocky swiped some of the snow off one and saw it was an ancient washing machine. There were more snowy cubes, tumbled about like dice in the toy chest of a giant child, and more snow-covered mounds scattered in every direction.

"This place is a dump," said Rocky. "Like, actually a dump. Not a metaphor."

"I think you're right." That supported my it-was-a-rat theory.

We trod between piles of ancient computer junk and office supplies and leaped over some metal rods, following the trail of whatever animal had scooted by.

"Look." She pointed at some animal tracks, the first clear prints we'd seen: broad feet with webbed toes. "It's an otter!" She beamed.

We followed the tracks along a frozen creek to the ledge of the embankment. The creek widened and turned into a waterfall, also frozen, cascading down to a pool of ice.

"It looks like it jumped," I said. We peered over the edge. The embankment was steep, and it was a long way down.

"I hope it's not hurt," said Rocky.

"Maybe it climbed down. Look." I pointed at horizontal slashes on the embankment. "This looks like a ladder."

"The otters must have made it," she said.

"They can do that?"

"They're really smart," she said. She softly whacked me in the arm. "They must use this thing all the time. That means they live here! That one we saw wasn't a fluke."

"So it's a great place to set up the ottercams?"

"Exactly."

It did seem perfect. The place was deserted, except for the otters. I couldn't believe our luck. We took some of the metal rods we'd already seen, and some cinder blocks to brace them.

"We can use some of that wire to attach the cameras to the poles," I said. I squeezed past a sun-bleached metal sign leaning against some rotting lumber. My shoulder swept part of it clean, revealing Sid—. I knocked the rest of the snow off.

SIDNEY'S DINER, it read. HAMBURGERS AND MALTS.

"It's from the restaurant we just saw," said Rocky. She was right. There was no kangaroo on the sign, but they did have the line on it about Sidney's being home of the famous pocket burger. "I wonder how old it is?"

"Old," I said.

"There's this reality show about guys finding junk and selling it for a lot of money," she said. "I bet that sign is worth a hundred bucks."

"*American Pickers*," I said. "I watch it, too." I felt a little thrill. We had something in common! "I don't think we could carry that thing home, though."

"Good point. Let's just set up the cams."

We posted a camera by the woodpile, and another by the pool. Rocky started setting one up by the waterfall.

"We have one more camera," I said.

"How about there?" She pointed at a road zigging and zagging down the embankment to the river, about forty feet from the waterfall. "If you pointed it at the cliff, we could see the otter going up and down the ladder."

"Perfect." I headed down the road. As I came around the first bend, I realized there were the ruins of a building at the bottom, with ragged, fire-blackened walls and one corner disintegrating into rubble. There were smaller buildings behind it, run-down and deserted. I felt a chill that wasn't due to the weather. Something terrible had happened here. I decided not to go any closer. I placed the pole there at the curve and rigged up the camera pointing toward the hollow where the icy waterfall crashed into the pool.

I was startled by a crunch of metal behind me. I whirled around but couldn't see anything. It was probably a piece of junk shifting in the wind. Still, I was overcome by a panicky feeling and hurried back up the path.

"What's wrong?" Rocky asked.

"Nothing. I just realized I should get home."

We took turns crawling under the fence and started back up Half Street, treading in the tracks we'd made earlier.

"That was fun," said Rocky. "I can't wait to see the video. It's going to be awesome."

"Yeah," I agreed, but I didn't mean it. Whatever terrible thing had happened there sucked all the fun out of the adventure.

CHAPTER 4

"You're in big trouble," Penny said the moment I walked in. She slouched on the couch while puppets on TV yapped at each other.

"Isn't this show a little young for you?"

She shrugged. "Everything else is just as dumb. Mom's mad at you."

"Great." At least it wasn't Dad. I went up the stairs to the office. I could hear her mumbling the way she does when she's in the middle of a graphic-design project. She heard me and wheeled around in her desk chair.

"There you are. Where did you run off to?" She didn't sound *that* mad. Penny tended to exaggerate.

"We were looking for otter tracks by the river. We needed to go while the snow was fresh." I paused, realizing my mom had no idea why I would be chasing otters in the first place. "It's our science-fair project this year."

She squinted at me. "Oliver agreed to do something about otters?"

"Not Oliver. Rocky from next door."

"Really?" she said. "You're doing something without Oliver?"

"I'm sick of robots."

"Well, I was supposed to meet a client, but you left me with Penny. Lucky for you the client postponed because of the snow."

"If there was no snow, we'd both have been in school and you could have gone."

"Good point. Well, now I need you to stay home with Penny and fix lunch."

"No problem."

"I'm glad you made a new friend," Mom said. "Oliver's a good kid, but you need a bigger circle."

"Yeah." Was Rocky really a friend, though? Where would we be after the science fair? I thought about it as I plodded downstairs. Penny was now sitting upside-down on the coach—legs up on the back, arms sweeping the floor.

"Do you want to build a snowman?" I asked her.

"Hmmm. Can we build a snow *woman*?"

"Of course."

So we went out and started rolling snow. Penny decided the snow was too full of dirt and leaves for a good snowperson, so we built a fort instead.

"This will protect us," she said.

"Protect us from what?"

"Extremists," she said, which made me wonder what was going on in the puppet show she'd been watching. We built three walls, about two feet high. I carved out a hole in the big pile of snow while Penny rolled snowballs and prepared a pile of ammo. There was enough room for us both to hide if an army of extremists stomped up the lawn.

That evening I checked the camera website for updates. There was only one snippet of video. The footage was a rectangle of darkness, nineteen seconds long. I'd forgotten that you had to put the cameras in well-lit areas if you wanted to see what happened at night. I saw a flash of some bright, silvery dots waving in the darkness. I watched the clip again and again, trying to make sense of it, but couldn't. Maybe it was moonlight reflecting off some shifting junk? In any case, it wasn't an otter.

I logged out, then spent a half hour Googling "ruined buildings in North Minneapolis," with no success—if the information was there at all, it was buried under all the stories about the tornado last summer. I couldn't ask Mom and Dad without them asking their own questions, like how did I know the ruins were there in the first place.

Rocky was out at the bus stop the next morning.

"I saw you playing with your sister yesterday," she said. "It was really cute."

"Thanks." I felt myself redden.

"So, is there any new video?" she asked.

I shook my head. "Nothing useful." I'd checked again that morning.

"Oh well. We'll get some soon. Hey, can you tell me how

to check it myself?" The bus door opened, and she jumped on. I got on right behind her, and we ended up sitting next to each other. When Oliver got on at the next stop, he raised his eyebrows in an annoyingly meaningful way.

I didn't talk to him until second period, social studies. "Hey." I took my usual seat next to him.

"Don't you want to sit next to your girlfriend?" he asked.

"Oh, knock it off, Ollie." He hated being called that, and I only used it when I wanted to annoy him.

"Sorry, Jimbo." He pretended to look at his textbook until class started.

The teacher, Ms. Holtz, came in looking grim.

"If you'll all be quiet," she said. "If you'll all be quiet!" she said again, this time louder. Ms. Holtz was never loud. It surprised everyone into shutting up.

"I have some important news about one of your classmates." Her voice was hoarse. "Dmitri Volkov is missing. His parents haven't seen him since yesterday."

The whole class turned to look at Dmitri's empty desk, their faces puzzled.

"If anyone knows anything, please go to the principal's office. The police are there now, trying to figure out . . ." She stopped when a chair squeaked against the floor. Oliver stood up and shoved his books into his bag, zipped it up.

"Oliver, do you know something?" Ms. Holtz asked.

"I saw him yesterday afternoon," Oliver said. "I don't know anything, but I saw him."

"Go, go." Ms. Holtz waved at the door.

Oliver shouldered his bag and left. Everyone was so quiet, the only sounds were his footsteps, then the door opening and closing. He didn't come back to class.

Kids were whispering about Dmitri for the rest of the day. Most said that Dmitri had fled town after committing a crime: he'd beaten someone up, robbed a store, or stolen a car. Possibly all three. A kid at lunch said he'd heard about the disappearance the night before. His brother knew Dmitri's sister. He said that Dmitri had definitely done something bad, and that he'd run away before. Last time he'd been found in Kansas City with a duffel bag full of stolen golf balls. "He was selling them on the street," the kid said. Maybe he got part of the story wrong, but he wasn't making it up. Selling golf balls on the black market in Missouri? Who would make that up?

I checked the camera website as soon as I got home. There were three new clips of video, but none of them were of otters. Each was just a blur of snow and shadows flickering into nothingness.

I had a sickening feeling. The cameras had been stolen. Those blurry clips were the cameras being jostled as they were grabbed from behind and turned off.

So much for fate being on my side.

I watched each of the clips again, but couldn't see anything to confirm my theory.

I looked again at the clip from the night before—there was no new video from that camera. Maybe the thieves had found that camera in the night, the one closest to the fence, and had come back today for the others. I watched the clip a few times. I kept noticing the four fluttering dots of silver, tiny bright moths in the sea of shadows.

I paused the video when the dots were on the screen, took a screen shot, and opened Mom's photo-editing software. I pasted the screen shot into the canvas, then went to the image settings and increased the brightness and contrast until a shape emerged. Two shapes, actually: a pair of feet. The camera was pointed down, toward the woodpile, so it made sense that that was all they would get. It was enough to ID the thief, though.

The silver dots I'd seen were the metallic tips of bootlaces. The laces themselves were black, threaded into boots that were equally black, barely visible even with the contrast cranked up. But I'd seen those boots before. In fact, one of those feet had crushed my toe and nearly removed a pinkie toenail.

The boots belonged to Dmitri Volkov, Oliver's science-project partner—and missing person.

CHAPTER 5

I caught Oliver at his locker before lunch the next day. I hadn't had a chance to talk to him since social studies the day before. He'd been off-line all night, probably because he didn't want people asking him about Dmitri—which was exactly what I wanted to ask him about.

"Did you tell Dmitri about the ottercams?" I whispered.

"I didn't know it was a secret."

"So you admit you told him?"

"You only *admit* things you're ashamed of," he said. "I didn't do anything wrong."

"You told a known thief we had expensive cameras lying around, ripe for the taking."

"You don't know that he's a thief."

"You don't know that he's *not* a thief."

"You're a fine one to talk," he said, shutting his locker. "Unless you got permission to use those cameras in the first place."

I realized people were eavesdropping, pretending to look for something in their lockers or check their text messages.

"Never mind," I whispered. "I have something to show you. Can you come to the library?"

"Sure," he said. "We'll miss lunch, but I'm sick of everyone looking at me anyway."

We went to the library, logged into my email, and opened a picture I'd stored there.

"This was taken by one of the cams." I traced the outline of feet with my finger. "These are boots." I pointed at the silver blobs. "You can see metal bootlace tips there and there, and there."

"You mean aglets." Oliver knew the words for things I didn't know had words.

"Whatever. They're metal." I dropped my voice lower. "Do they remind you of anyone?"

"Lots of people wear boots. Boots usually have laces. Laces always have aglets."

"Not like these," I said. Dmitri's aglets were oversized and heavy. When he didn't double-tie his bootlaces, you heard them rattling in the hallways. The ones in the picture were the same. "I bet that's Dmitri. I think he stole my cameras."

"Great. If he turns up, you can ask for them back." He stood up and grabbed his backpack.

"That's my point. This could help us figure out what happened to him. He was at the junkyard sometime before he disappeared."

"So tell the police."

"I want to go look, first," I said. Maybe there were footprints, or something. "Can you come with me after school?"

"No."

"Come on, Oliver. You're in this, too. You told Dmitri about the cams."

"So what?"

I decided I was going about this the wrong way. "Look, I could use your help. You're way smarter than me. If there is a clue, you'll see it. I won't."

"So we're playing Hardy Boys? What do you hope you'll find, a crumpled-up train schedule?"

"I don't know."

"Why didn't you ask Nancy Drew?"

I figured he meant Rocky. "She's got debate practice. Come on, Oliver. It'll only take twenty minutes. I don't want to go alone." He still wasn't convinced. "Come on," I pleaded. "You know how my dad is."

"*Fine*. I'll go. I'm going to grab lunch." It was too late. The bell rang before he got to the door.

Oliver pulled the chain to stop the bus as soon as we were over the bridge. "We might as well get off here," he said. "It's closer."

"All right." We got off with a couple of other kids on First Street and walked until we saw the neon kangaroo. A shabby-looking guy watched us through the window of the Laundromat. He might have gone in to escape the cold. It was the kind of cold day that makes your skin freeze up and turn to leather.

We headed down West Bank Road and took a left on

Half Street, stepping carefully in the trails Rocky and I had stamped down a few days ago so our shoes wouldn't fill up with snow. The snow was too deep to make out tracks, so I couldn't tell if anyone else had used those trails. Oliver was quiet except for his labored breathing in the cold air. We passed under the railroad bridge and came to the fence.

"What we do about this?" he asked.

"We go under." Somebody had pulled the tree branch out of the gap, making more room to climb under the fence.

"You didn't tell me about this part," said Oliver. He took off his backpack and tried to figure out what to do with it, finally unfastening one of the arm straps, feeding it through the fence, and reattaching it. I did the same with my own backpack.

I crawled through first, and pulled the flap back the other way so Oliver could crawl in. He stood up and dusted himself off.

"So where are the ottercams?" He followed my old tracks toward the curving path down the embankment. No, not *my* tracks. Dmitri's flat-soled boot tracks. Oliver stopped at the steep incline.

"I know where we are," he said in a strange, hollow voice. He ran on ahead, skidding on an icy patch and regaining his footing.

"Oliver?" I hustled to catch up. By the time I did, he was at the first bend.

"I knew it," he said, staring at the burned ruins.

"What?" I asked him. I realized we were standing by one of the camera posts, but it had been knocked over. I picked up the metal rod. The wire I'd used to attach the camera to it had been neatly snipped. It wouldn't have been hard to untwist the wire, but why bother if you had wire cutters?

"Dmitri must have had wire cutters," I said absently.

"Yeah, he took some of my tools," said Oliver. His voice was calm, almost disinterested.

"'Took' borrowed, or 'took' stole?"

"I don't want to talk about wire cutters," he said. "Do you know where we are, Jim? Do you know what you dragged me to?"

"No." I dropped the pole.

"Did you wonder what those buildings were?" Oliver asked.

"Of course I wondered. I tried to look it up, but it was no use."

"Jim, this is the site of Nomicon."

"Nomicon?"

"The place my dad worked."

"Oh." If I'd ever known the name of the place his dad worked, I'd forgotten about it. It didn't come up much because his dad—

"Oh," I said again.

"This is where my dad died," said Oliver.

CHAPTER 6

We crawled through the gap in the fence and headed back up Half Street, Oliver lagging behind. I turned back around a couple of times to make sure he was still there. When we passed under the railroad bridge, I saw that he'd stopped, was trembling and crying.

I went back. "I didn't know," I told him, reaching out to nudge his elbow. How could I? I'd never been to Nomicon.

He yanked his arm away and let loose with a torrent of swearwords and accusations. The gist of it was that I shouldn't have dragged him there, and that I was a jerk for doing so, and there were lots of things I could do next, and/or things he would do to me. His voice rose and mixed with the roar of a train rumbling overhead.

"Oliver, I didn't know where we were," I told him when the train had passed. "I never would have made you go there if I'd known."

"So you ended up there completely by accident?"

"We were just trying to find the otters."

"You and your fuzzy otters," he said. He really did say

"fuzzy otters," and it was funny. I laughed, and then he snorted and laughed, too. It hurt to laugh in the cold air.

"I never did get lunch," he said. "Let's try that burger place up there. The one with the kangaroo."

"Pocket burgers," I said. "Sure."

The restaurant was roomier inside than it looked. We sat at a table by the front window, and I watched a street sweeper brushing away the dirty slush on the shoulder of First Street. Oliver picked up the laminated menu and stared at it.

"I wonder if it's made from real kangaroo meat," I said.

"They aren't made of kangaroo," he said. "They're pocket burgers. Sam's in South Minneapolis calls them stuffed burgers. Victoria's Grill in Saint Paul calls them inside-out cheeseburgers. They're all the same thing."

"We were here first!" someone called out, before I could explain to Oliver that I'd been joking about the kangaroo meat. For the first time I noticed the guy behind the grill. He was tall and lanky and wore an apron. "All those places arguing about who had the first inside-out this and stuffed that," he said. "My granddad did it first. I can prove it."

"We'll take your word for it," said Oliver. "I'll have a Sidney's classic with fries and a Coke."

"Me too," I said. It would spoil my supper, but I was famished.

"Sorry again," I told Oliver after we got our Cokes. "I didn't know that's where your dad worked."

"I didn't recognize it right away, either," he said. "I thought it was further away."

"Everything seems a long way away when you're little."

He slurped up about half his Coke. I did the same. Being really cold makes you thirsty for some reason.

"I can't believe they never cleaned up the site," he said.

"Me neither."

"Better than putting in a strip mall. At least people aren't eating burritos where my dad died. Or getting their nails done."

"Sure. Yeah."

It was getting dark outside. It must have been past five o'clock, because people were starting to come into the restaurant straight from work. It got noisy with men—they were all men—men talking about contract jobs and uptight customers and zoning ordinances and malfunctioning machines.

"Nineteen fifty-five." The cook plopped burgers down in front of each of us, and a basket of fries.

"We have to pay already?" Oliver reached into his pocket.

"No, 1955 is when my granddad opened this place. Sam's came along over a year later." He shook his head. "They got everybody fooled, mainly 'cause nobody cares what happens up here on the north end."

"Four Sid Classics and a pitcher over here, Sid!" said one of the men at the table next to us. The cook cut his history lesson short to go throw more meat on the grill.

I took a bite from the burger, and my mouth filled with burning-hot, gooey cheese and diced onions.

"Ack. Hot." I took some ice from my Coke and sucked on it.

"You have to let it cool," said one of the guys at the table next to us.

"Yeah. Thanks," I said around the ice cubes. I recognized him from somewhere.

"You kids are Panthers," he said, pointing at my chest. I looked down.

"Oh yeah." I was wearing my school sweatshirt.

"I went to Wellstone, too," he said. "Back then it was called Stinson, but Panthers are Panthers. Hear us roar!"

"Hear us roar," I agreed. I knew where I knew him from—he was the guy from the excavation place. I remembered his snow tennis game with the lumberyard next door.

"Dan Clouts," he said. "Clouts and Sons."

"James Knox. This is Oliver."

"If you kids are Panthers, you're all right by me." He paused. "Hey, you must know that missing kid?"

"Yeah."

"Was he a friend of yours?"

"We're in the same classes. He was the last one to see him." I pointed at Oliver, who was shaking his head furiously. He wanted me to shut up.

"Holy cow," said Dan. "I'm sorry about your friend, guys. I hope he's OK."

"Me too."

Suddenly a man got up at a different table. He was a

young guy, tall and muscular, wearing denim coveralls from a service station. His eyes were bloodshot and rimmed with dark rings. He looked at Oliver and me, then at Dan, then at me again.

"What do you know about Dmitri?" he asked.

I gulped. "Nothing."

"So you don't need to talk about him." He sat down again, his friends nodding.

"Your burger's getting cold," said Oliver in a low voice.

"I'm letting it cool," I whispered back.

"It's cool now. Eat it so we can go."

I ate the burger quickly, barely tasting it. I didn't realize until the last bite that it was much better than the ones at Sam's.

"I'm done," I told Oliver, stuffing the last bit of burger into my mouth. He was finished with his and looking out the window. A train was chugging by, so the cars on First Street were backed up.

The place had gotten so busy, Sid hadn't had a chance to drop off the check, but Oliver took some bills from his pocket and counted them out. He could remember the prices of things, compute sales tax, and add it all up in his head. He reached down.

"I forgot my backpack," he said.

"Oh. Mine too." We'd been in such a hurry, we'd left them back on Half Street, the straps threaded through the fence. We'd have to go back, and this time it would be dark.

* * *

It was even colder now, too, with a harsh wind blowing. We started down West Bank Road, but Oliver stopped.

"I can't go back there," said Oliver.

"You don't have to. I'll get both bags."

"I'll wait here," he said.

I trudged on alone, in the dark. West Bank Road was brightly lit, but once on Half Street I was plunged into darkness. I knew when I was there by the gleam of moonlight on the fence, and it took some groping around in the dark to find the backpacks.

I worked my own backpack free easily. I hadn't pulled the strap through the clasp; I'd just tied the two ends in a clumsy square knot. I pulled the other strap over my shoulder and went for Oliver's backpack.

There was a flash of blue light beyond the fence, low on the ground. I stared ahead, seeing nothing in the blackness of the old dump other than the glint of moonlight on snow and metal. I couldn't imagine what that flash might have been. I wanted to be out of there, ASAP.

I fumbled at the strap of Oliver's backpack. He'd redone the clasp, and I realized I'd have to take off at least one glove and let my hands get chapped raw in the wind.

The light flashed again, and then a steady yellow beam shone right at me. As I worked the bag free, there was a scrape of metal near the gap in the fence. I turned and ran. It was awkward, swinging two backpacks and trying not to skid and fall on the packed snow. There was a flash of blue light at my heel. I tried to run faster, my chest aching as I took in deep breaths of freezing air. I didn't slow down until I reached the concrete pylons at the start of Half Street.

Oliver was waiting for me in front of the restaurant, jumping up and down to keep warm. He looked like the neon kangaroo hopping along behind him. The same shabby man watched us warily through the window of the Laundromat, like he knew we'd been up to something.

CHAPTER 7

We walked briskly, neither of us talking. I didn't tell him what happened. Even if I could work my half-frozen jaw, I wasn't sure what *had* happened.

"Want to come in and thaw out?" he asked when we got to his place. All I could do was nod. When we came in from the subzero cold, the warm house felt like a sauna. I kicked off my snow mocs and unzipped my coat.

"Is that you?" Oliver's mom called from the kitchen.

"Yes!" Oliver called back.

"Both of 'em," said a man sitting in the recliner.

Oliver peered blindly into the living room through foggy glasses. "Peter?"

Peter Clayton was Oliver's mom's on-again, off-again boyfriend. They were supposed to be off-again for good a few months ago, but here he was.

"Hope you're hungry," said Peter. "Your mother's making tacos."

"Great," said Oliver. His mom couldn't have known he'd come home with a stomach full of hamburger and cheese. He took off his glasses and huffed on them, pulled out a tail of his flannel shirt to wipe the lenses.

Oliver's mom came out of the kitchen. "So where were you two?"

"Working on Jim's science project," said Oliver.

"Well, you could have checked in," she said. "With that other kid gone missing . . ."

"Of course. I'm sorry," said Oliver. "We didn't expect to be gone so long."

"Your parents are worried, too," she told me. "Your father called."

"OK." I felt a sense of impending doom. "I better go." I zipped up my coat and dug out my hat and gloves.

"Let me drive you. It's cold out there." Peter got up and grabbed his coat and hat. "Be right back, Ellen!" he hollered to Oliver's mom.

His car was an Audi A7. It started up quietly, even in the bitter cold. The dashboard lit up, soft and blue. The seats were heated. An iPod Touch was cradled in the center, playing a sixties song. Peter drummed in time on the steering wheel.

"Nice ride," I said.

"I splurged," he said. "Only way a California boy like me can get through these winters."

Peter taught engineering at the U, but according to Oliver he was loaded, with patents and high-tech stocks. For that matter, Oliver was loaded. Oliver's parents and Peter all used to work together.

I gave him my address, and he headed up Victory Drive. He drove slower than he had to.

"Ellen told me you and Oliver know this missing boy," he said.

"Not that well."

"But he visited Oliver just before he went MIA?"

"Yeah."

"Does this have anything to do with you and Oliver disappearing for a few hours just now?"

"No," I lied.

He turned onto my street, pulled over, and turned off the stereo.

"I noticed the way you cringed when Ellen said your dad called."

"I cringed?"

"I couldn't help but notice. I think maybe you're in more trouble than you're admitting."

My dad has a short temper. He yells a lot, and sometimes he goes off the rails. He hollered at me for over an hour once because of spilled ketchup. Another time the police came: I'd been on the computer when I was supposed to be watching Penny, and he'd made so much racket the neighbors called.

It wasn't just me. He'd blown up at neighbors for letting their dogs crap on our lawn. He'd gone off on clerks at stores and attendants in parking lots. He'd gotten out of his car to confront drivers at red lights. After he lost his job at the security company, he started taking anger-management classes. He reads books and does homework. He's gotten better.

I wondered if Peter knew all that from Oliver or just figured out I was in deep doo-doo? He was a smart guy.

"I'm not trying to bust your chops," said Peter. "Oliver is like a son to me, and you're his best buddy. I care about you guys. So I just want to know if everything is cool."

"It is. We're totally cool. But thanks."

"I know you're good kids, but back in L.A., I saw some good kids get mixed up with bad stuff, you know?"

"Yeah, but we're not mixed up with anything."

"Glad to hear it."

"Thanks for the ride."

"Anytime," he said.

Mom and Dad were waiting for me in the living room.

"Nice of you to drop by," said Dad.

"Sorry I'm late," I said. I hung up my coat, glad I had a reason not to look at him. "I was working on a school assignment and was gone longer than I thought. I forgot my cell phone at home."

"Well, since that other kid went missing, it's not a good idea to forget your cell phone, or not bother calling," he said. "Parents get ideas."

"I'm sorry. I didn't mean to worry you."

"He's safe. That's what matters," said Mom. She gave me a hug.

"Find a way to call," Dad said. "Borrow a cell phone. If you can find a pay phone anymore, call collect."

"OK." I started for the stairs.

"Not so fast," said Dad. I stopped. "I need to talk to you about the storage shed."

"What about it?" I asked, hoping that it was what an innocent person would ask.

"The security cameras," he said. "I'll show you. Let's go." I went up the stairs, my legs like Jell-O. Dad was right behind me.

We went into the office. He got on the computer and navigated to the website for the cameras. I felt a surge of panic, not remembering if I'd logged out last time.

I must have. The log-in window appeared; Dad entered his own info and clicked through to a list of a half dozen cameras, each showing a thumbnail view of our house from a different angle. I didn't know he had the place wired, but I should have known.

"Here," he said, clicking one. I saw a dirty white hill. "This camera is hidden in the trunk of the cherry tree. It's the only one with a view of the shed. You dumped snow in front of it. It can't see jack."

It couldn't see Jim, either, I realized. Otherwise, I would be toast. I'd piled the snow up in front of the tree the day before I stole the cameras.

"I didn't know it was there," I told him.

"I guess you couldn't," he said. "But I need you to clear a path."

"Will do." How many times would I have to shovel the same snow? I wondered.

"I have a lot invested in that equipment," he reminded

me. "I cashed out my retirement to start this business. It was the only way to keep this family afloat."

"I know."

"Good. That's all." He closed the browser without logging out. "Do you need dinner? Your mother made tuna casserole."

"I already ate."

"All right. You probably have homework," he said. He left the office.

I went back to the camera site. Dad was still logged in, so I checked out his other cameras. I watched clips of me shoveling the walk, of me and Penny building a snow fort.

I glanced back at the door and decided it was safe. I logged out of the site as Dad and logged in as me. There were no new clips.

There was a noise behind me. I closed the browser window—too late, because whoever was there could have seen it already—and turned around. Dad was back.

"Phone call for you," he said, handing me the receiver. "It's the police. They found the missing kid from school."

PART II
CELESTE

CHAPTER 8

The officer asked a lot of questions: Did I know Dmitri? How did I know him? Where did we go to school? I answered as best I could. Dad waited, listening to my end of the conversation.

I had plenty of questions, too—like where did they find him, and how was he doing, and did he have any digital cameras in his pocket. Not that I would have asked that last one with Dad hovering nearby, but I didn't really get a chance to ask *anything*.

"Do you know a man named Theodore Whaley or Ted Whaley?" the officer asked me.

"Nope."

"You've never met or heard of a Ted Whaley?"

"Never." Why did she think asking the question in a slightly different way would get a different answer? "Who is he?"

"He's a person of interest in this case," she said mysteriously.

"Am I a person of interest?" I asked.

"Perhaps."

"Why?" Even if they'd found Dmitri with one of the cameras in his pocket, they wouldn't be able to trace it back to me. Could they? And was it technically stealing if you took something from your own house?

"Dmitri Volkov asked for you," she said after a long pause. "He wants to see you and a boy named Oliver Newton. Do you have any idea why he'd want to talk to you two?"

"No."

"Well, if you want to see him, he's at North Memorial, Room 508. And if you think of anything else you forgot to tell me, please give me a call." She gave me two numbers, which I scribbled on a Post-it pad.

I had to sit through another mini-interrogation with Dad, who was as skeptical as the cop that I didn't know why Dmitri wanted to talk to me.

The next day was Saturday. Monday was MLK Day, so I had a three-day weekend. All I wanted to do was sleep until Tuesday morning, but Dad woke me up before nine.

"Oliver's here," he said.

"Who?" At first I thought he said "the officer's here," because I'd been interrogated all night in my dreams.

"Oliver? Your best friend?"

"Oh, right." I got dressed in yesterday's jeans and sweatshirt and headed downstairs. Oliver was waiting in the foyer, still wearing his coat.

"What's going on?"

"You must not have got the message," he said. "I'm going to see Dmitri. He's asking for us. I figured you should go, too."

"Yeah, sure." Shoveling would have to wait. So would breakfast. I stepped into my snow mocs and grabbed my coat. "Is your mom giving us a ride?"

"No. Peter is."

"He's already at your house this morning?" I asked as I snapped up my coat.

Oliver gave me a look.

"Oh. Right." We went out into the cold. "He's a nice guy," I said.

"He is," Oliver agreed. "Did you tell the police anything?"

"Nah. I didn't want to get Dmitri in trouble, especially when he's in the hospital."

"Me neither. Same reason."

Peter barely nodded at me when I got in. He was bobbing his head to the beat of a Beach Boys song. I sat in the back and melted into the heated seat, thinking about beaches and sunshine.

Based on all the movies I'd seen, I expected Dmitri to be lying in bed, hooked up to a hundred machines and barely able to talk. He was actually sitting up and reading, holding his paperback awkwardly with bandaged hands.

"Oh, hi." He put the book down when he saw us. "Thanks for coming. Sit down." There was only one chair, and Oliver took it.

Dmitri's face was windburned and looked scabby. I glanced at the title of his book—*Caught Stealing*. The cover showed bloody hands against a chain-link fence. "My brother got it downstairs at the gift shop," Dmitri explained. He shifted in bed, made a pained face, and drew a deep breath. "He said it was the only book down there that didn't suck. He was right. It doesn't."

"Good title," said Oliver.

Dmitri smiled with one side of his mouth. "Yeah, I get it."

"So you're not going to deny it?" Oliver asked.

"No. I took your stuff. I'm sorry."

"It's all right," I said. It was hard to be mad when he was bandaged up, taking labored breaths, and wincing every few seconds.

"No, it's not all right," Oliver muttered.

"Um—so are you going to be OK?" I asked Dmitri.

"Mostly," he said. "Maybe I'll lose a couple of fingertips on my left hand." He flexed it lightly. "And the top parts of my ears. Your skin turns black in the cold. Did you know that?"

"Read it somewhere," said Oliver. "I've never seen it for myself."

"It's not pretty," said Dmitri. He took another deep breath.

"We'll take your word for it," I said. "Did it happen in the abandoned junkyard?"

Dmitri nodded, then shook his head. "It only *looks* abandoned," he said. "I took one of your cameras and was heading for the next one when someone got me from behind."

"What do you mean, got you?" Oliver asked.

"I got Tased. I got knocked out."

I thought of the bolt of blue electricity that nearly hit my heel.

"How long were you out?" Oliver asked.

"I don't know. My memory is a little shaky."

"How did you even find the cameras?" I asked him.

"I got lucky." He looked at his hands, realized what he'd said, and laughed, then winced.

There were voices in the hall, coming our way.

"I'm sorry I lost your camera and your tools," Dmitri said quickly. "But don't go back there. That's why I asked for you. I had to warn you. That place isn't safe."

"We already went back," said Oliver. "It was deserted."

"Look, I'll find a way to pay you back for your stuff. Just please don't go back."

"We won't," I assured him.

A minute later, the room was full of people: a guy around twenty years old, a girl who was about sixteen, and a round-faced boy who was about ten.

"You two were at the pocket-burger place," said the twenty-year-old. "Why are you stalking my brother?" I recognized him. He was the one who'd confronted us at Sidney's. Now I could see Dmitri's face in his.

"Don't be a jerk, Sergei," said the girl. He turned to her, his nostrils flaring. The little boy hid behind her.

"Back off, Masha. I just want to know what they're doing here," he said.

"I *asked* them to come," said Dmitri.

"Well, I never saw them before," said Sergei. "My brother goes missing, then I hear these strangers talking about him, then they show up at his hospital room. . . ."

"They're good guys," said Dmitri. "It's OK."

"All right. Well, I need to talk to you alone," said Sergei. "Masha, bring Lexy to the coffee shop. I promised him a donut."

"But we came to see Dmitri!"

"Ten minutes! Sheesh." Sergei waved us all out of the room. "You two, as well. Clear out for a while."

"We're leaving anyway," said Oliver. "I am sorry about what happened, Dmitri."

"Me too," I added.

"Thanks a lot," said Dmitri. "See you guys at school."

"I'm going to ask if I can go it alone on the science-fair project," Oliver added. "I hope that's cool."

"Sure." He raised a bandaged hand to wave goodbye. I had a lot more questions, but Sergei was looking at us impatiently and Oliver was my ride.

"Thanks for coming," said the girl as we walked to the elevator. "Dim doesn't have many friends."

"No problem." I punched the button for the elevator. "Your name is Masha?"

"Only my family calls me Masha. It's short for Malasha. This is Alexei." The boy looked at us with wide blue eyes, but didn't say a word.

"I'm Jim, and this is Oliver."

The elevator arrived with a ding. An old man was there, in a wheelchair, with tubes in his nose and a nurse behind him with some equipment. We crowded in.

"I'm sorry Sergei was such a jerk," said Malasha. "He's been really stressed, worrying about Dmitri."

"It's understandable," I said.

"Where did they find Dmitri?" Oliver asked.

The man in the wheelchair nodded. He was curious, too, even though he didn't know who we were talking about.

"He was sleeping on the floor at a Laundromat. The guy who works there found him last night, curled up in a corner."

"Is his name Ted Whaley?" I guessed, remembering the man the officer had asked me about.

"That's him," Malasha confirmed. The elevator stopped on two, and the nurse wheeled the old man away. He looked back at us sadly, wanting the rest of the story.

"Is it the Laundromat on First Street?" I asked. We'd walked right by it.

"That's the one."

"How long was he there?" Oliver asked. "He was missing for forty-eight hours."

"We're not sure," said Malasha. "The guy who found him isn't the most reliable witness."

The elevator dinged for the ground floor. We got off as people squeezed past us to get on. Alexei started tugging on his sister's hand and moving toward the coffee shop. "See you later!" said Malasha as Alexei dragged her away.

"Do you want to get back on Team Robot?" Oliver asked. "Since your otters are dead in the water. Um, sorry for using that expression."

"I don't know." The fact that I still had to do a science-fair project was the last thing on my mind.

"You can help build the robot this time," he said. "You're right. It shouldn't be just arts and crafts."

"Yeah, but that's what I'm good at. Remember my paper-plate turtle from second grade?"

"That turtle rocked," he said.

We found Peter in a lounge by the gift shop, working on his laptop. He shut the screen, but not before I caught a glimpse of his Web-browser window: diamond rings against a field of robin's-egg blue.

CHAPTER 9

I knew I had to tell Dad about the cameras. The longer I waited, the worse it would be.

I decided to do the shoveling first. I started clearing out a gap between the cherry tree and the shed, careful not to dump snow into Penny's fort. It felt good to work, and to get everything else off my mind for a while. I was halfway done when Rocky came over.

"Hi," she said.

"Hi." I was breathing hard from the shoveling. Clouds of white puffed from my mouth. "If you're here to ask about the ottercams, I have some bad news. They were stolen."

Her mouth made a little "oh" as the news sunk in. "What did your dad say?"

"Um . . . I haven't told him yet."

"He didn't even know you took them, did he?" She reached out and took my wrist with a mittened hand, looked at me with wide brown eyes. "I should never have put you up to this, Jim."

"You didn't hold a gun to my head."

"I know," she said. "That's not important. I can pay for half. I mean, I don't know if I can, but I should, and I'll find a way."

"Thanks," I said. I slowly pulled my arm away. "Anyway. Our project is finished."

"Do you want to do something else?" she asked.

"I was thinking of helping Oliver with his robots. Since his partner didn't work out."

"Didn't work out? You mean disappeared?"

"He's back. We went to see him at the hospital." I told her he'd been attacked, but not where it happened.

"If you see him again this weekend, tell him I'm glad he's OK," she said.

"I don't think I will, but sure. Anyway, he's not up to the robot project, so I told Oliver I would help him. Sorry."

"All right," she said, not the least bit upset. "I'll figure out something else."

I watched her walk home, already feeling like I'd just made a huge mistake. When I turned back toward the house, I saw a puff of yarn the size of a tennis ball bob above the snow pile and disappear again.

"Penny?"

She clambered out of the hideout. "I heard. You stole some cameras and now they're gone."

"Don't even try to blackmail me. I'm going to tell Dad myself."

"What's blackmail?"

"Ha. If you look up *blackmail* in the dictionary, there's a picture of you."

"Well, I don't want to blackmail you this time. I don't even want *you* to tell."

"I have to, Penny. It'll just get worse if I don't."

"Jim, he's going to be so mad. He's going to yell. A *lot*."

"I know."

"If you promise not to tell, I'll . . ." She stopped, unable to think of anything. She was usually on the other end of blackmail. "I'll finish shoveling for you, and I'll shovel the rest of the winter."

"No deal."

"I won't ask you to do anything else ever again."

"Yeah, right."

"He's going to kill you," Penny whispered somberly.

"Come on, Penny. Dad yells, but he never hits anyone."

"Nobody's ever done anything this bad."

"Good point. But I still have to tell him. I'm going to do it as soon as I'm done out here."

"You are such a dummy!" Penny ran up the back path, through the door, and slammed it behind her before I could respond.

I finished shoveling and went inside to tell Dad what happened. He was pointing out something to Mom in the neighborhood newspaper, trying to talk her into something. I wouldn't make it worse by interrupting their conversation. Dad hated being interrupted. Anyway, I might as well enjoy my last five minutes of Internet access. I'd probably be banned from anything good for the rest of my life.

I went upstairs to the office. The computer was on, the browser logged into the camera site. When was the last time I'd been logged in? Could I really have forgotten to log out? I went closer and saw that a map was open in a separate browser. There were four pushpins in the map, each with a number. The map just showed a gray area, but I could tell what it was by the river on one side and the roads on the other: it was where Nomicon used to be.

I started to piece together what was going on.

"Penny?" I went down the hall, saw that her door was open and her room was empty.

I ran downstairs, grabbed my coat, and was out the back door before Mom and Dad could ask what was going on.

I hustled down the bike path toward the river. About twenty cars passed me before I got to the park. I expected every set of headlights to belong to Dad's car. I ran across the street against the light. The neon kangaroo at Sidney's was still hopping along. It would be a nice place to warm up if I found Penny. *When* I found Penny.

I walked down West Bank Road and turned left at Half Street. It was early afternoon, but the junkyard was already full of shadows.

"Penny, are you in there?" I wrapped my fingers through the fence and shook it. "Come out! It's over! Never mind the cameras!" I sighed, and slipped through the gap in the fence. I really didn't want to go in there.

"Penny!" I shouted again. I spotted a small set of boot prints to my left, weaving among piles of junk. I followed them to the otter slide, then along the embankment to a stand of trees and bushes. This was where the cameras *had* been, not where they were now.

I stubbed my toe on a large metal pipe embedded in the ground. I heard claws scrambling inside. An animal darted out of the pipe and raised itself, chattering at me, daring me to take another step forward. It was about two feet tall, with glistening chestnut fur. An otter! I heard more chattering and skittering echo. Otters were nesting inside the pipe.

I backed up, crashing into someone. We both screamed.

"Penny!" I could have strangled her. I hugged her instead. "What are you doing here?"

"The camera site lied," she said. She showed me a printout of the same map I'd seen. "I figured out where to go, but none of the cameras are where the map says they are."

"What are you talking about?"

"I beeped the cameras," she said.

"What?"

"I beeped the cameras," she said. "I forget the right word, OK?"

"You mean you traced them?"

"Yes. You just click the button that says 'locate my cameras.'"

I didn't even know you could do that.

"How did you log in?" I asked her.

"I used your email address and guessed the password," she said. "Jim, plus sign, Rocky."

"Oh." Was I that obvious? "I just used that because it's for our project."

"Sure you did. Well, the site lied, because I don't see the cameras anywhere."

"Never mind," I told her. The site must be using the last known data. Penny had gotten a map of where I'd placed the cameras the first time. "It isn't safe here, and it's getting dark. Let's go home."

I helped her through the fence and we started back up Half Street. No blue bolts of electricity this time.

"Jim, do you believe in robots?" Penny asked.

"Of course I believe in robots. They're not like fairies. We know robots exist."

"Yeah, but this one probably doesn't," she said.

"Which one?"

"The one I just saw," she said.

"You saw a robot that doesn't exist?"

"I saw a robot," she said. "Back there at the junkyard. It was a big lizardy robot."

"Maybe you just saw something that looked like a robot." I glanced back at the fence and the piles of snowy debris. Who knew what was lurking there?

"I'm too tired to walk home," she said. "Can we call Mom and get a ride?"

"Sure. We should call anyway, just to let them know we're OK." The only problem was I'd left my cell at home again. "We just need to find a phone."

The first two businesses we saw were closed, but the third was open—the service station. Webber Automotive. "We repair imports!" the sign boasted.

The door rang a bell as we came in. There was nobody there, so we waited a moment. A man came in, wiping greasy hands on a towel.

"Sorry, we're not technically open—" he started saying. "Oh, it's you."

It was Sergei Volkov.

CHAPTER 10

He gave us a ride home in the tow truck, all three of us in the front. I gave him the address, and he turned onto First Street, stopping for a train.

"Listen," he said. "I'm sorry I was mean to you this morning."

"No problem."

"Dmitri told me what happened," he said. "You need to know, my brother's not a thief. He's never been in trouble before. He just acts retarded sometimes."

"You're not supposed to use that word," said Penny.

"Yeah, there's lots of stuff I'm not supposed to do." The train passed, and Sergei headed up the avenue. "So, I'd make Dmitri give the stuff back, but somebody stole it from him." He found our street and turned. "Dmitri doesn't need to get into real trouble. It would kill our mom and dad to even know. Dmitri is the good one."

"If he's the good one, why did he steal?" Penny asked.

"I think he was trying to prove a point." He pulled over, a couple of houses short of ours.

"Prove what?" I asked.

"That he's a re—that he's a dimwit," said Sergei. He glanced at Penny. "Can I say dimwit?"

"I think so," she said.

He reached into his pocket, came up with a handful of bills, and shoved them at me.

I thumbed through the bills. There were lots of ones and fives, and a few tens and twenties.

"That's probably not enough to pay for everything that got stolen," said Sergei. "But it's all I got right now. Don't tell anybody what happened, OK? Especially don't tell anybody who might tell the police. Did you tell your mom and dad?"

"Not yet."

"Then don't." I realized that the money wasn't compensation. It was a bribe, with the hint of a threat on the other end.

"They were my dad's cameras," I told him. "He'll find out sooner or later, and when he does, he'll ask me a bunch of questions, and I'll have to answer."

"Listen," said Sergei. "I'll try to replace the cameras, all right? See if you can hold out a week or two."

"Really?"

"Just keep your mouth shut."

"He will," said Penny. She shoved me out the truck door before I could think things over.

Mom was waiting for us.

"Where were you this time?" She sounded more exasperated than angry. "Penny disappears; you go stamping out the door without telling us where you're going. Now your father's out looking for you both."

"We're fine," I said. "Sorry." I tried to come up with an alternative explanation and floundered.

"We were fighting," said Penny. "Jim said that I couldn't use the computer, even though he wasn't using it, so I logged in anyway and got on Facebook as him and posted a few updates."

"I don't care what it was about," Mom interrupted. "Jim, we need you to act more responsible. Your sister is only nine. Don't let her goad you."

"Sorry. I was mostly kidding around." I looked like an idiot, but at least Penny came up with a story—and in genius Penny fashion, came up with something Mom didn't even want to ask questions about.

"Who was the guy in the tow truck who just dropped you off?"

Uh-oh. She'd seen that.

"The brother of a friend from school," I told her. "He saw us walking back and gave us a ride."

"Right. Well, as long as you know him and didn't take a ride from a stranger."

"Mom, we're not stupid," I said.

"I know, I know. Let me call your dad. I'll ask him to stop at the store so he has time to cool off."

"Sorry," said Penny. "We didn't mean to make him mad."

"Oh, I know you're both going to act like kids sometimes.

Maybe this business with the missing boy will help him appreciate that you don't get into *real* trouble."

At least not yet, I thought.

That night Penny and I made a robot. We used tinfoil-covered boxes for the body and a cookie tin for the head. The legs were a wrapping-paper tube cut in half.

"Is this robot a boy or a girl?" Penny asked when the robot was nearly finished.

"Neither. Robots are its."

"I think it's a girl." Penny gave the robot unruly rainbow hair made of used gift-wrap ribbons. "The robots I saw earlier were definitely boys."

"You saw more than one?"

She looked at me. "You said there weren't any robots."

"I didn't say that."

"Forget it! They don't exist!" She wagged the robot's wire arm to make it wave. "Hi Jimmy," she chanted in a high-pitched, robotic voice. "My name is Celeste."

"Don't get too attached to it," I told Penny. "Oliver's robot is going to smash this thing to pieces."

"No!" Penny protested. "You can't hurt Celeste!"

"Never mind." I patted Penny on the arm. "You can keep this one."

"Yay!" She moved the arms up and down into different poses. "Can we make her do things?"

"Like what?"

"Walk and talk and beat up other robots?"

"I don't know how," I said. "We'll have to bring in an expert."

Oliver came over the next day with a book and a plastic box full of electronic bits and pieces.

Dad was in the living room watching a football play-off game. Green Bay was at Philadelphia. He was rooting for the Eagles because his second-favorite team was whoever was playing the Packers. Oliver glanced at Dad, then at me, raising his eyebrows inquisitively. I got his meaning and shook my head: No, Dad still didn't know about the cameras.

"So what did you bring us?" Penny peeked in the box.

"Lots of gadgets and doodads and whatsits," said Oliver. "Enough for a half dozen rudimentary robots."

"Awesome! What's this?" Penny picked through the box and found a plastic thing about the size of a deck of cards. It had a blank LCD display.

"It's the logic controller," said Oliver. "You use it to program the robot."

"Program her to do what?" Penny asked.

"Whatever you want," he said. "I'll show you." He started making a squidlike thing with the logic controller at the center and wires for tentacles, lecturing while he worked: The sensors were like our own senses, responding to light, sound, or touch. They sent messages to the logic controller, which was like the brain. The logic controller decided what to do according to its program and triggered the actuators, which were like muscles. They made things work: flashing lights, wheels, whatever.

"What if I want her to talk?" asked Penny.

"You have either a playback mechanism or a TTV device—text to voice." He tapped Celeste's cardboard body. "Does she come apart?"

"Sure."

I thought Penny would protest, but she watched in fascination as Oliver disassembled Celeste and punched pinholes in her body so he could thread the wires through until just the tips were visible.

"This is just like when you were in the hospital," I whispered to Penny.

"Shut up. No it's not."

Oliver ignored us. He attached a mesh square about the size of a postage stamp to the end of each wire, and secured them with a few drops of wire glue.

"Usually I'd solder," he said. "But this is good for more flammable robots." He taped the controller inside the box and put Celeste back together. I had to respect how quickly he worked, and how neat the results were—the squares were evenly spaced around Celeste's body, two on each side of the box. It made her look more robotic. Celeste also seemed better put together—more balanced and less likely to fall apart at the joints.

Oliver led a couple of wires down one of her tubular legs. He attached the first wire to a small button and glued it to the back of Celeste's ankle. He plugged the other wire into a plastic ring with wheels around the rim and secured it to the robot's feet. "This is an omni-wheel," he explained. "*Omni* mean all. An omni-wheel gives your robot the ability to roll in any direction."

"Celeste," Penny told him.

"Sure. Celeste." He set the robot on the table, turned her on, and let her roll toward Penny.

"Cool!" Penny reached for her, but Celeste abruptly veered away. Penny's eyes popped wide. I held out a hand to catch the robot, and Celeste turned again, heading back to Oliver. Oliver sent her back to me, and I sent her back to Penny.

Penny trapped the robot so she could pick it up. "I love it! How does it work?"

"Ultrasound sensors," said Oliver. "If something is coming closer, the sensor is activated, and the logic controller tells the omni-wheel to change direction."

"That's all there is to it?" I asked.

"That's all there is," he said.

Sensor, controller, actuator. All that time I thought this stuff was way over my head, but it suddenly sounded doable.

I checked the camera website later that night. Penny had a good idea, "beeping" the cameras. Maybe I could track them down. I wouldn't have the guts to confront somebody, but I bet Sergei would.

Amazingly, there were dozens of new five-second

fragments from all four cameras. The GPS data indicated they were still at the junkyard. Most were close-ups of junk: the first zoomed in on a bent-up sign, the second captured the logo from a bicycle frame, the third showed an embossed symbol on a refrigerator door. Y, A, W.

Strung together, they made words!

I clicked through the thumbnails, writing down the letters recorded on miscellaneous signs, inked markings on old wood, accidental letters made of twisted metal. What I got was an incantation from an ancient language.

YAWA YATS YAWA YATS

Then I remembered that the videos appeared with the most recent on top, so they were showing up in the opposite order of how they were recorded. The actual message was:

STAY AWAY STAY AWAY STAY AWAY

Whoever had taken the cameras knew I was watching and was sending me a message. I didn't care who they were. I intended to do what they said.

CHAPTER 11

I had a friend request from Malasha on Monday morning. She messaged me as soon as I accepted it.

Malasha: Happy MLK Day.
Jim: You too.
Malasha: r u doing anything?
Jim: Nope.
Malasha: Dmitri is home. He's doing better. Come over later w/your pal Oliver?
Jim: I'll try. Where do you live?

Jim: Want to see Dm? His sister invited us. Hoping your mom or Peter can drive.
Oliver: Peter can't drive us b/c his car was stolen.
Jim: WHAT? WHEN? WHERE?
Oliver: On the street in front of our house.
Jim: Tell him I'm sorry. Srsly. It's a nice car.
Oliver: I will. Anyway, I can't go. ttyl.

Jim: Going to see Dmitri. Want to go?

Rochelle: To the hospital?

Jim: He's home now.

Rochelle: Hm. I really don't know him at all.

Jim: Me neither. His sister asked me to come. I don't think he has many friends.

Rochelle: He doesn't. Doesn't seem to want any.

Jim: So, want to go? I don't want to go alone & I have to talk to you anyway.

Rochelle: Ooh, mysterious. Sure.

It took two buses and an hour to get there. There was no straight route. We had to go downtown and transfer.

"So, talk to me about what?" she asked when we were on the second leg of the trip.

"I was wondering if you were going to do the otter thing without me."

"I don't think so. Why?"

"Because I've been thinking. I don't think it's safe. There were some metal barrels. I bet you they're filled with toxic waste." That part was a lie, but I needed to keep her out of there. "And the signs said Keep Out."

"No worries," she said. "I'll do something else."

"Cool." I pulled the rope to stop the bus. "We get off here."

The Volkovs' house seemed to sag at the corners. There was a new Cadillac Escalade in the driveway, freshly washed and out of place.

"Wow. I wonder what his dad does?" The SUV probably cost even more than Peter's A7.

"He's a limo driver," said Rocky. She pointed at a subtle decal on the back window: Lowry Limousine Express, Ltd. Followed by URL and phone number.

"Of course." The fancy car was his business. Maybe it was worth it to drive around in style.

As if on cue, Mr. Volkov came out of the house. He was an older version of Dmitri, in a dark wool coat and aviator glasses. He nodded at us. The mirror shades and the overcoat and the luxury SUV probably accounted for the rumor that he was a mobster. He looked the part—more crime boss than hired thug.

"You're here for Dmitri? He's inside." He had an accent. I wondered how long the Volkovs had lived in the U.S. He climbed into the car and backed out, the Escalade barely making a noise as he rolled it out onto the street.

Rocky elbowed me. "You're crushing on the Caddy?"

"Yeah, I might get one myself. I should ask him how it drives compared with a Lexus RX."

"Buy me a Prius while you're at it."

"No prob."

The porch was crowded with boxes of mysterious engine parts and car trim. We navigated through them to rap on the front door. The silent ten-year-old answered the door, giving us one look before wandering off again, leaving the door open so we could come in. A cartoon blared on the TV. Alexei stood watching it, rocking from foot to foot.

"Hey." Dmitri limped downstairs, dressed in jeans and a Packers sweatshirt. One pants cuff was rolled up, giving him a lopsided look. He hadn't shaved his head, so he had a peach-fuzz layer of hair on his scalp. He seemed smaller and more normal without his tough-guy boots.

"Hey, how are you?" I asked. I had to shout to be heard over the TV.

"Better," he said. He showed us a bandaged hand. "I get to keep my fingertips."

"Glad to hear it."

"They're still numb," he said. He shouted into the living room. "Turn it down, Alex!"

The boy found the remote and lowered the volume a notch, his eyes still glued to the screen. A parrot was on the screen jabbering in Spanish. The set was high-definition, good enough to see the pixels from the computer-generated animation.

"He loves this show," Dmitri said. "He doesn't understand a word. Come on. Masha made tea." We followed him into the kitchen—heaps of onions and turnips and beets in bowls on the counters—very homey. Malasha was there. We traded hellos, and she went to the living room to watch Spanish-speaking parrots with Alex.

"Want some?" Dmitri filled a china cup—a dainty one, with flowers, that looked odd in his bear paw of a hand. "It's good."

"Something hot would be nice," said Rocky.

"Sure," I said.

Dmitri filled two more of the china cups and passed them to us. The tea smelled of oranges and cloves. It felt Christmassy, somehow.

"Tea is a big part of Russian culture," said Dmitri. He sounded like a social studies lesson. He realized it and grinned. "Well, it is. Cheers." He tipped his cup at us, and we tipped ours back at him and drank. It was good. I drained the cup and waited while Dmitri and Rocky sipped theirs.

Through the window I could see two cars covered with tarp. Dmitri saw me looking.

"Serge restores and resells cars," he explained. "He also does some repair jobs. You into cars, too?"

"He loves cars," said Rocky. "He's all Escalade this, RX that."

"You have expensive taste," Dmitri said.

"Hey, a guy can dream." I wasn't that much into cars, but I went with it.

"You should see Serge's '69 Mustang," he said. "He restored it using all original parts and trim. Come on, let's go look at it."

"Will he mind?"

"Oh, he'd flip, but he doesn't have to know," said Dmitri. He saw our faces. "I'm kidding, mostly."

His boots were by the back door, and when he slipped them on I realized why he looked lopsided. One of his legs was a bit shorter than the other. Hence the rolled-up pants cuff. Hence stepping on people's feet—he was off balance. The boots hid it well—one had a thicker heel.

"Serge made these," he said. "He said my ortho shoes made me look 'retarded.'" He winced at the word. "Even with Alex being who he is, Serge says that. But he did good with the boots. Come on."

"What does he mean about Alex being who he is?" Rocky whispered.

"I don't know," I whispered back. "I just know he never talks." There was more to it than that—the wide-eyed way he looked at the world, the way he seemed detached from everything.

We went down the steps into the backyard. There were more boxes of engine parts, car doors, and hoods leaning against the house. The whole house was like a repair shop. Dmitri peeled back the tarp on one of the cars.

"This is the Mustang. She's nearly done." The car was bright red with a blue stripe running down the middle. It looked amazing. It could have been driven straight from the lot in late 1968 and into the Volkovs' backyard.

"How long did it take Sergei to do this?" I asked.

"Since he got back from—since he got his job at the repair shop," said Dmitri. "He puts every penny he earns into this thing. All he has left is the interior." He pulled the tarp back down.

"Amazing work," I said.

"He'll make a nice profit, too," said Dmitri. "If he can bring himself to sell it. He loves this car."

He headed toward the back door, Rocky right behind him. I lingered, looking at the other covered car. The shape seemed familiar, and I had a feeling about it. I went over and lifted the front of the tarp.

"Hey, leave that one alone!" Dmitri shouted. It was too late. I had the tarp up enough to see the grille, a white hood, and the four trademark circles of an Audi.

CHAPTER 12

"Sorry." I dropped the tarp. "Just curious."

"It's not Serge's car," said Dmitri. "He does work for people on the side." He stood at the back door, holding it open, until I went back inside.

Malasha and Alexei were still watching cartoons, so we sat in the kitchen, draining the teapot. I managed to keep a poker face while Dmitri and Rocky talked about school, sports, and music, but all I could think about was that car in the yard. It was the same make, model, and color as Peter's stolen car.

Maybe Sergei was a car thief. He knew all about cars and could probably hot-wire one—if car thieves still did that. He'd admitted he'd been in trouble before. On the other hand, he was mad at Dmitri for stealing, so that didn't make sense. It also didn't make sense for me to get him in trouble when he was going to get *me* out of trouble, especially if he was innocent.

Rocky was nudging me. ". . . since this guy bailed on me," she was saying.

"Huh?" I'd missed whatever they were talking about.

"We could do something together," said Dmitri. It took me a moment to realize they were talking about the science-fair project.

"Sure," said Rocky. "What do you want to do?"

"I still want to build a robot," he said. "Oliver got me interested in the idea. I'd like to try it, but I can't handle tools right now." He held up his scarred hand.

"No problem," said Rocky. "Dad made me learn a bunch of guy stuff. I've used power saws, welding torches, you name it."

"We need a hypothesis," said Dmitri.

"I have one," said Rocky, her eyes shifting toward me. "Our hypothesis is that our robot can beat up Oliver and Jim's robot."

Jim: Any luck with Peter's car?

Oliver: Nope.

Jim: ☹

Oliver: The car is insured.

Jim: Still stinks.

Oliver: Yeah. He's pretty bummed.

Jim: BTW, we have a new mission. Dm and Rocky are sci fair partners. They're making a robot to fight ours.

Oliver: Srsly?

Jim: Srsly.

Oliver: Bring it.

* * *

In science class on Friday we spent most of the period working on our projects. Oliver worked on graph paper, sketching elaborate plans for robots. His lines were sharp and clean. He rambled while he talked about infrared detectors and weighted cudgels. I kept glancing back to see Dmitri and Rocky chatting. It seemed everything he said made her laugh.

Dmitri had been the center of attention all week, swarmed by kids with questions. He must have liked the attention, because I'd even seen him smile a couple of times.

Oliver was explaining about cudgels—that was what he called the robot's fists—and anchoring the robot so it could pack a punch. Mentally I traced the chain of events: An ultrasound sensor would tell the robot an enemy was at hand. It would send a signal to the controller, and the controller would trigger the actuator.

"How does it know where to punch?" I asked. Ultrasound told it something was near, but would the robot just flail randomly? Could it be strategic? Could it go for the gut?

"Good question," said Oliver. "We can use infrared cameras to give the robot an image of the combatant."

"You can do that?"

"Yeah, some of the newer sensors are amazing."

I sneaked another peek at Rocky. She was still giggling. Since when had Dmitri been so funny? I wondered. Oliver noticed I was looking.

"What kind of robot do you think they'll build?" he asked.

"Some kind of vehicle," I guessed. "Dmitri is into cars."

"Like an armored tank with a brain?" he said. He sketched one while he talked, barely aware he was doing it. "We'll strategize around that. See if you can find out more."

"Find out how?"

"Talk to Rocky," he said. "Make like it's just friendly talk."

"Of course." I'd been promoted from arts and crafts to being a spy.

Usually Dad meets customers on their own turf, but once in a while a client comes to our house. There was one on Friday: Dad had the case out and was discussing the various makes and models of security cameras. I had an instant panic attack and almost didn't notice who he was talking to.

"Hello, Jim!" he said.

"Peter. Hey." I noticed that the table was piled high with boxes. Every one had a picture of a camera on the outside. The end was nigh. "Sorry about your car," I muttered.

"It's insured." He waved it off. "But the incident has raised my concerns about the state of the neighborhood." He turned to Dad. "No offense."

"None taken," said Dad with a nod.

"I figured it wouldn't hurt to bolster the security. It's not about my car; it's about Ellen and Oliver. They're practically family."

"I know," I said.

"Are you and Ellen—" Dad started.

"We're very old friends," Peter interrupted. He removed a checkbook from the inside pocket of his corduroy jacket. "How much will all of these be?"

"Do you want all eight?" Dad asked, barely able to mask his excitement. It was a big sale.

"Sure," said Peter. "If it's worth doing, it's worth doing right."

Dad started jotting numbers down on an order form. My mind raced. When Peter realized some of the boxes were empty, he could accuse Dad of ripping him off. I had to say something. I just wished I didn't have to do it in front of Peter.

I blurted out my confession. "Some of the cameras are missing."

Dad looked like I'd just hit him in the face with a frying pan.

"What?"

"I borrowed a couple—a few of the cameras, and I, uh, I lost them."

"You *borrowed* some?" Dad asked. "And *lost* them?" He was just short of exploding, I knew, and would have if there hadn't been a customer sitting there and a big sale on the table.

"It was for a school project," I said. "I'm sorry. I know it was stupid."

"Don't listen to him!" Penny cried from the top of

the stairs. She ran down, her eyes flooding with tears. "Jim is trying to cover for me, but it was my idea. I took the cameras to play a joke on Maggie and it didn't work and I lost the cameras and I told Jim because I was scared to tell you!"

Dad rubbed his temples and took a deep breath. His eyes went from me to Penny, back to me.

Peter smiled awkwardly and took control. "Well, why don't we see which boxes have the cameras?" He opened a box and peered inside. "This one's good." He set it aside and reached for another.

"Why don't you do that, and I'll go see if I have any more in the shed," said Dad.

"Go right ahead," said Peter, reaching for a third box. He peered inside. "So far so good."

"Jim?" said Dad. He got up and headed toward the back.

"Yeah. I'm coming." I followed him. The sun was setting over the roofs across the alley, blinding us both.

"You better have a damned good explanation," he snapped. "Whether you're telling the truth or covering for your sister."

"I don't, but I can tell you what happened."

"Well, it'll have to wait." He unlocked the door. "It's bad enough to steal, but to humiliate me in front of a customer?" He opened the door, entered the security code, and quickly sorted through the boxes. There were no more of the 3G cameras here, which he probably knew. He just wanted a moment to yell at me. He slammed the door, closed and locked it.

"Come on. Let's see what the damage is." He strode back toward the house. I paused a second, feeling the icy wind cut me to the bone.

When we got back inside, the boxes were lined up neatly on the table.

"There must be a mix-up," said Peter. "All eight boxes have cameras."

"You're sure?" Dad opened a box, saw a camera, and set it back. He started to reach for another.

"Yes," said Peter. "I checked them all. Just let me know how much I owe you. I kind of have to get going."

Dad handed him the bill, his face a mixture of confusion and relief. "Hey, do you want bags for all this?"

"I'll get them!" Penny said. She ran into the kitchen. She was back a split second later with two grocery bags and started packing the cameras herself. "I found the kind with handles," she said.

"Thanks," said Peter.

"There's no wiring needed with these 3Gs, so they're easy to set up," said Dad. "But if you need help placing or mounting them, give me a call. No charge."

"Will do," said Peter. He put on his coat and grabbed his laptop case. "Jim, can you help me out here?" He nodded at the grocery bags.

"Of course." I grabbed the bags and followed him out of

the house. A black BMW was on the street. It beeped at us as Peter unlocked the car.

"Loaner," he explained. "Just put that stuff in the backseat. So who's covering for who?" he asked after I put the bags in.

"Penny's covering for me," I admitted.

"I can pay you back. It'll take a while, but I'll find the money."

"Jim, I know your dad is hard on you," he said. "If I can ever keep a kid from harm, I will."

I wanted to correct him, to tell him my dad might yell a lot, but I was never unsafe. I didn't, because what if he changed his mind?

"For what it's worth, my dad was pretty rough, too," said Peter. "Nothing I ever did was good enough. Straight As, scholarships, math fairs. I still wasn't man enough for him. If I got in a fistfight to prove I was tough enough, he would yell at me for losing."

"Wow." I knew Peter had grown up poor, in a bad part of Los Angeles, but it was hard to imagine him in a fight. "I'm sorry. And thanks for this."

"You will need to pay me back," he said. "I have plenty of money, but it wouldn't be in your best interest, long-term, to not have any consequences. I'm sorry for your situation, but it's no justification to steal. Besides, I see you as a kid with potential. Not a charity case. We can work out a payment plan, OK?"

A kid with potential. Potential for what, I wondered?

Mom and Dad said stuff like that all the time, but it felt weightier from Peter. Parents and teachers were supposed to tell kids they were full of potential. Peter sounded like he meant it. I wanted to ask him what potential, because I sure didn't know.

"Jim?" Peter nudged me. "How does that sound?"

"Good. Great. Thanks." I offered him my hand.

"Your word is all I need," he said, and didn't shake it.

"One of you used the cameras without permission, and the other one is lying," Dad said when I went back inside. "But you *both* embarrassed me in front of a customer."

Either because Penny was involved or he was relieved the cameras were there after all, or because his anger-management classes were working, he only yelled at us for about half an hour.

We both lost TV and video-game privileges for two months, and neither of us would see any allowance until further notice. I was just glad he didn't ban me from using the computer—he must have figured I'd need it for school, which I did.

Rochelle: I saw u & ur dad when I walked by your house. You were out at the shed.

Jim: Yeah. Ugh.

Rochelle: He found out about the cams?

Jim: Sort of. Yeah, but it's all right.

Rochelle: Are you sure?

Jim: Yep. I have a guardian angel. Hey, do you want to hang out this weekend?

Rochelle: Can it be on Sunday?

Jim: Sure.

Rochelle: You do know it's the Super Bowl, right?

Jim: I forgot, but I don't care that much about football.

Rochelle: Great! How about we go to the megamall? It won't be that busy b/c of the game.

Jim: Smart. OK.

Oliver: Peter has this place monitored like a maximum security prison.

Jim: I know. He bought the cams from my dad.

Oliver: My mom doesn't like it. Says she feels like she's being spied on, even tho she's the only one w/the password to the website.

Jim: Our place is cammed to the max too. I think Peter means well. Nice guy. Just got freaked when his car was stolen. Thinks he's protecting you.

Oliver: I know. He's madly in love w/my mom. Want to work on the robot Sunday?

Jim: No, I have plans. W/Rocky.

Oliver: Srsly? A date?

Jim: I don't know. Maybe it's a date.

Oliver: Don't forget to ask her about her robot.

CHAPTER 13

"I thought you were grounded," Mom said when I brought up the mall. I'd waited for Dad to be gone to ask permission.

"Not exactly," I said. "Dad just said I can't watch TV or play video games." I'd never been grounded. The only place I ever went was Oliver's house, anyway, and they thought he was a good influence.

"OK, you can go," said Mom. "But please take Penny."

"What?"

"She hasn't been able to do anything fun in ages," Mom explained. "I should make more time for her, I know, but I've had so much going on."

"But we'll have to do Penny stuff," I complained. I didn't especially want to go to Build-A-Bear Workshop.

"You're lucky I'm letting you go at all. Bring your sister or stay home. Your decision."

"All right, all right. I'll bring her."

When I thought about it, bringing Penny wasn't a bad idea. I kind of owed Penny something after the whole camera fiasco. She hadn't blabbed, and she hadn't tried to blackmail me. She even tried to cover for me. Also, Rocky had seen me with Penny before and said it was cute.

We met Rocky at the bus stop. She was wearing a nice suede jacket she'd never worn to school.

"You aren't cold in that?" I asked.

"I hate wearing a parka at the mall," she explained, hugging herself to keep warm. "I thought I'd suffer now and be more comfortable later." Maybe that was all it was, and maybe she wore shiny lip gloss to keep her lips from getting chapped in the icy wind, but the whole effect was that she looked really cute. My head spun and my mouth was dry.

If she thought it was weird I'd brought my little sister, Rocky didn't say anything. On the ride to the mall, Penny told her all about Celeste and how her next robot would talk to her and clean up her room and zap the mean kids at school.

Rocky laughed. "Let me borrow it when you're done."

"Is there a robot store at the mall?" Penny asked.

"No, but we can look at the Lego Store." I remembered Oliver telling me about the kits he'd used when he was younger. "I think they're kind of expensive, though," I warned her.

That would have been a good chance to ask Rocky about the robot *she* was making, but Penny moved on to other topics—school, unfair teachers, kids who thought they were all that, and why it was bogus that she couldn't have a puppy.

Rocky told Penny about some puppy videos she'd seen on YouTube and promised to send her links.

The mall wasn't as empty as we hoped. Everybody must have gone because they thought it wouldn't be busy just before the Super Bowl.

"So what do you want to do?" I asked Rocky.

"Amusement park!" Penny shouted.

"I don't have money for that," I told her. "Besides, I was talking to Rocky."

"I have passes to the aquarium." Rocky dug into her handbag. "My dad got them somewhere. I only have two left, but it's cheaper for kids under twelve. We can split the cost of Penny's."

"Sure," I said.

"Yay!" said Penny.

Once we were in, we walked slowly through the wide tunnel past the serene tanks full of fish, crabs, and sea horses. The aquarium was busy, and we stuck close together. Penny laughed at a gigantic turtle. Rocky wished out loud that they had otters, like the aquarium in Duluth. We fell quiet, watching the abundance of sea life circling in the eerie blue light of the tanks.

We got to the sharks just in time for feeding. The toothy predators made short work of a bucket of bloody chum. Penny said it was disgusting and moved on. I found her at another tank, the crowd cleared away because of the shark show. She pointed at a rock and some seaweed.

"He's hiding."

"Who's hiding?"

"Look!" She poked at the glass with her finger. I stared at the rock but couldn't see anything special. A moment later, an octopus emerged and lazily floated away from the rock. His long legs made a brief balloon, then kicked and sent him zooming away.

"Wow," I said. It was weirdly beautiful.

"Yeah," said Rocky. I hadn't even noticed she'd slid in next to me. "It looks like an alien." Her hand fluttered near mine. Did she want to hold hands? I'd almost worked up the courage to find out when we were interrupted by a hubbub behind us. We turned and saw a boy on his back, kicking the ground. He was having a seizure.

"Oh no," said Rocky. The overhead lights brightened. A security guard said something into his walkie-talkie, then yelled at the crowd to stand back. Rocky cut in front of him—he halfheartedly swiped at her elbow, but Rocky got past him and started talking to the boy's mother. No, it was the boy's *sister*. It was Malasha, and the boy was Alexei.

The mall security offices had a nurse on duty. Rocky and Penny and I waited outside in the hall. Some uncomfortable chairs were bolted to the floor near a row of lockers.

"Is he going to die?" Penny asked in a hushed voice.

"No, he just had a seizure," said Rocky. "He has epilepsy. Dmitri says a lot of autistic kids have multiple diagnoses."

"Scary," said Penny.

"It is, but he'll be OK."

Poor kid, I thought. I also thought, Rocky knows a lot about Dmitri's family all of a sudden.

"So, have you been hanging out there a lot? Working on your science project?" I asked.

"That, and I've grown close to Dmitri," she said.

"Close," I echoed.

"We're kind of, you know."

"Yeah," I said. All those giggles and brushed elbows in science class weren't my imagination. "How come he didn't come with us?"

"He's a Packers fan, so he wanted to stay home and watch the pregame stuff. He knows we're here. He's totally cool about it."

"Of course."

Once the thrill of a crisis faded, Penny was bouncing literally off the walls. She'd jump up on the chair, hit the wall with both hands, and spring back. Rocky looked at her phone, punched in a message. Must be texting her boyfriend, I thought. She finished and put the phone away.

"I gave Masha and Alex a couple of passes for the aquarium earlier today. I wasn't sure we'd see them here, but they're here because of me, you know? I should wait for them."

"No problem."

"*You* don't have to," she said. "That's the thing." She nodded at Penny. "She's going nuts."

"Do you want to meet up later?"

"I'll go home with those guys," she said. "Sorry. I know this wasn't much fun."

"It's all right," I said, even though there wasn't much right about it.

I took Penny to the food court. She inhaled a crepe with hazelnut spread and raspberry syrup. I poked at my own, but I wasn't hungry for it. A big ball of self-pity was taking up all the room in my stomach. Rocky and Dmitri were "kind of, you know."

"Can we look at robot kits?" Penny asked when she'd finished her own crepe and half of mine.

"Sure."

We went to the Lego Store. They had small robots you couldn't program, and a big one that you did program. Penny scowled at the box, which showed what looked like a muscle-bound robot dude carrying a gun. "Celeste is better," she said. "Why don't they make girl robots?"

"They should," I agreed. I was relieved. We could never have afforded the robot kit, and I didn't want Penny to have her heart set on it.

Penny noticed a sign on the way out and pointed at it. "Look!"

ROBOT BATTLES
MALL OF AMERICA ROTUNDA
Saturday, February 25 10:00 AM

Compete in three categories!

Ages 8–12

Ages 13–17

NEW! Autonomous robots (all ages) NEW!

(NO REMOTE CONTROLS OF ANY KIND ARE ALLOWED IN THIS CATEGORY)

Enter as individuals or teams of two.

Winners in each category receive a $1000 prize!

Sponsored by the Lego Store and Albatross Electronics

"Can we enter?" she asked. "Please?"

"I'm not eight to twelve," I reminded her. "You'd have to enter by yourself."

"No, I want to enter Celeste in the all-ages category!"

"I don't know." We were beginners at this, and Celeste was still made of cardboard.

"I want to do it!" she said. "Oliver gave us a bunch of supplies, and we have the book. Please? I want a girl robot to enter and beat everybody."

I wondered if we'd be able to build a robot all by ourselves. Even Celeste was made with Oliver's help.

"Come on," she pleaded.

"Sure. Fine." Sensor, logic controller, actuator: it wasn't that hard.

CHAPTER 14

"I don't get it," said Oliver. He squinted at my sketches, which were a blur of erased and redrawn lines. We were in class, discussing our projects. Dmitri and Rocky were there somewhere, I supposed, but I hadn't looked for them.

"It's a collapsible robot," I said. "When it senses the enemy is coming, it folds up and hides." I was sure that Oliver would hate the idea, but I'd decided to show it to him anyway. He grunted noncommittally and looked at the sketch again. "So it can make itself flat," he said. "What if the other robot rolls over it? What keeps the logic panel from getting smashed?"

"This would be made of metal." I pointed at the robot's head on the sketch. "It's shaped like a shallow bowl, see. When it collapses, the legs tuck underneath and support the top. Something could roll over the top without hurting it."

"Then what?"

"It jumps up and zaps the enemy."

"No zapping," he reminded me. "We agreed to voltage limits. It does need weapons, but I like the overall design."

"Wow. Thanks."

"There's only one problem." He pushed the notebook back at me.

"What's that?"

"I don't know how to build it."

We jumped on a city bus after school and went to see Peter.

The University of Minnesota had a mix of old-fashioned-looking buildings made of brick and crazy-looking modern ones with copper-plated exteriors. Peter worked in one of the modern ones. We walked through a misshapen atrium, down a slanted hallway, up a half flight of steps, and down another hallway. Peter's office door was open. A bushy-haired teenager was talking to him. He barely looked old enough to be in college. Maybe he was some kind of prodigy. Recurrent neural networks this, dynamic temporal behavior that.

"What are they on about?" I whispered.

"Robots that can learn," said Oliver.

Peter looked up. "Oh, hey. Come in, both of you." We did. I muttered hello, feeling sheepish for interrupting their talk.

"Oliver, this is Rolf Strauss," said Peter. "He's one of my new graduate students. He won this year's Elijah Baley fellowship." Rolf nodded politely at us. "And this is Oliver Newton Jr. and his buddy Jim," Peter added. Rolf's eyes widened.

"Your dad's work was incredible," he told Oliver. "It was a big loss to the scientific community when he died."

"It was a big loss to my family, too," said Oliver. That sucked all of the warmth out of the room for a moment.

"Rolf, tell Oliver about your research," Peter suggested. "He's interested in robots. He'll love it."

Rolf opened his mouth and closed it again. "I don't know how to explain adaptive robotics to a layman."

"It's good practice," said Peter. "Besides, Oliver . . . both of these guys are more than regular laymen."

"OK, I'll try." Rolf found the only blank corner of the board and wrote: ∀

"What's this?" he asked.

"An upside-down A," I ventured.

"What about this?" He erased it and wrote: ⅁

I looked to Oliver, but he obviously wasn't playing. He was scrutinizing the equations on the other half of the board. "A G, also upside-down," I said.

"OK, this," he said. He erased the second letter and wrote: W

"An upside-down letter M," I guessed.

"Not a W?"

"Well, the first two were upside-down, so I figured . . ."

"Exactly." He pointed the marker at me. "You saw me write two upside-down letters, and you started reading upside down. You adapted to the situation. It's hard to teach computers how to do that." He put the marker down. "Sure, you can teach them to shape-match inverted letters if you're expecting it, but if you *weren't* expecting it, the robot won't figure it out. A problem that's easy for a six-year-old to solve can stump the world's best robot if it wasn't programmed to solve it."

I looked at the letters, thought about a robot brain trying to make sense of the writing. "Does this apply to robot battles?"

"Of course," he said. "Especially in real military applications. It's essential to have robots function in unknown environments, and that's what my work is all about."

"Making robots do things they aren't programmed to do," Oliver added.

"Even better," said Rolf. "Making robots that can do things the programmer didn't think of. Robots that can even change their own program if the situation requires it."

"Great, Rolf," said Peter. "Very clear and succinct."

"Thanks. I'll find those journal articles." He put down the marker and headed out.

"That young man is brilliant," said Peter.

Oliver looked glum. Rolf probably made him feel the same way Oliver made *me* feel, but Peter didn't notice. "So, what can I do for you?"

"How would you build this?" Oliver showed my drawing to Peter.

"A collapsible robot! Interesting design," said Peter. "Why eight legs? It doesn't have a structural advantage over six legs."

"Just because," I said. Because it was an octopus, was why.

"Are these jointed segments, or do they telescope?"

"I don't know," I admitted.

"That's why we wanted your opinion," Oliver added. "The legs have to be strong, but very flexible. I don't know how to do it."

"You could use elastomeric polymers," said Peter, "but you won't find them at the hobby shop."

"Oh yeah. I read about those on the robot forums," said Oliver. "Can you get some?" I had a feeling it was what Oliver had been gunning for all along, but he'd wanted Peter to suggest it.

"Heck, I already have some," said Peter. "Let's go to the lab."

We went through a side door into a large room. Three tables were strewn with machine parts and gadgets. It was a robot maker's heaven. Peter rummaged around in a cupboard until he found a box, took it out, and handed us each a white plastic rod.

"This is a robot part?" I asked. It looked like a cross between a gummy worm and a bendy soda straw. I ran my finger along the length of it, feeling a long row of rings connected by webbing.

"Technically, it *is* a robot," said Peter. "It can function all by itself."

"Cool."

"How does it work?" Oliver peered through the pinhole at the end of his.

"You insert a single-pin connector into either end. The rings are multipurpose: touch sensors and actuators."

"Wow," I exclaimed. Peter glanced at me, surprised that I knew what he was talking about.

"Can we solder them onto a bigger machine?" Oliver asked. "And how do you program them?"

"You'd need a special conductive epoxy to attach them. I have some you can use. I also have a manual that has all the code you need to know. I'll email you a PDF."

"Thanks," I told him. "This is really cool of you."

"You're welcome," he said. "It's great to see kids excited about science."

"Why would Peter be so nice to us?" I asked Oliver on the bus ride home.

"He's a nice guy."

"Yeah, but this is above and beyond."

"Ah, these were just freebies for him. People give him beta stuff all the time. They're hoping he'll write it up for a journal and give them free buzz. It's a trade-off."

"I guess. But there's something else." I told him about the cameras, and how Peter covered for me. "Why would he do that?"

"Well," he said, "he might have sensed that your dad was a hothead and thought he was saving your behind."

"He did, sort of." Why would he *sense* that, though? "You told him about my dad, didn't you?"

"A long time ago," he admitted. "We were talking about stuff."

"So, he felt sorry for me?"

"He doesn't pity you," said Oliver. "He relates. He sympathizes. Anyway, don't worry about it. Peter is loaded. His professor salary is a fraction of what he makes. He has all those patents he split with my dad, plus a bunch more. He could easily quit his job and retire, but he really likes teaching."

"I still plan to pay him back," I said. I wanted to put the whole camera thing behind me, and I couldn't as long as I owed someone.

"Good luck with that," he said.

"I have an idea," I said. "But I need you to do something for me."

"What?"

"Nothing. I mean, I need you to do nothing. Let me create and program this robot all by myself. You can supervise, but I have to build it."

"How come?"

"Because I want to use the same robot for something else." I told him about the contest at the mall, and the thousand-dollar prize. "It has to be *my* robot, though. Otherwise I'm just letting you bail me out, the way Peter bailed me out." And the way Sergei *tried* to bail me out.

"OK. You can do it all. I'll just coach you. I think you can make a robot that beats Dmitri's robot. But you're going to be facing some pretty tough competitors at the mall."

"It's worth a shot."

"You'll be going up against kids who have been doing this for years, and are at the top of their game, and smarter than you to begin with."

I laughed. "Doesn't hurt to try."

"I mean me," he said. "I was already planning to enter."

The next day I got off the bus a few stops early and headed toward West Bank Road. I walked past the Laundromat and the flashing kangaroo, turning in to the parking lot of Webber Automotive.

"Is Sergei around?" I asked the guy at the desk.

"He's under a car right now," he said. "What do you need? I'm the owner, so if it's anything to do with a car, you can tell me."

"It's personal."

"Well, you can leave a note." He shoved a yellow legal pad at me, flicked a finger against one of the pens in the plastic pot on the counter.

"Is it all right if I wait?" I didn't want to trust a stranger with an envelope full of cash.

"If you want, but donuts and coffee are for customers only." He pointed out a few stale-looking pastries and a pot of coffee by the door that I hadn't noticed.

"No problem." I settled down in one of the red plastic chairs bolted to the floor. I dug through my backpack for the robot book, which I'd been reading in bits and pieces for the past couple of weeks. It was starting to make sense.

The owner grunted and disappeared into the garage. A moment later the door jingled. An old man came in and helped himself to a cup of coffee. He stank of sweat and cigarettes. There's no nice way to say it: he reeked. He put one donut in his pocket and grabbed another, then sat down next to me.

"Heya," he said. His voice was rough, and he barely spoke above a whisper. "Robots, huh?"

"Yeah. I'm trying to make one," I said.

"Hope it doesn't turn on you," he said as offhandedly as if we were talking about raising pit bulls.

"Ha."

"You think I'm kidding?" He leaned forward in his chair. "You know, they used to make robots right down the road there."

"Yeah. That was a long time ago."

He whispered right in my ear, suffocating me with stale donut breath. "A few of them are still around."

The owner returned from the garage, saw the old man, and rolled his eyes. "Look, Ted, we told you. This isn't AA. You can't just sit in here drinking our coffee and telling people your problems."

"It's four o'clock," said the old guy. "The Russian guy said I could come at the end of the day."

"Sergei doesn't run the place. I do."

"He said you just throw out the leftovers anyway."

"Bah, take what you want and get out of here," said the owner.

"Don't mind if I do." Ted took the last two donuts and refilled his mug, draining the pot. "This coffee is cold, you know."

"That's because we made it ten hours ago."

Sergei came through the door from the garage, wiping his hand on a towel.

"How's your brother?" Ted asked Sergei.

"He's fine."

"Glad to hear it."

"Yeah, thanks for dropping by every day to ask," said Sergei.

"The coffee's cold," Ted said again, jingling the door as he left.

Sergei came and sat next to me.

"Jim. What's up?"

"I don't need this after all." I took the envelope out of my jacket pocket.

"Come on, man." He pushed it back at me. "Don't go waving envelopes of cash around. I'm lucky Chuck didn't see that." His boss was going through a pile of papers and paying no attention to us.

"Sorry."

Sergei shook his head in disbelief. "Don't you know I'm on probation?"

"No," I said. I didn't know, but I wasn't that surprised. I shoved the envelope back in my jacket pocket. "What did you do?"

"Look, I'm glad Dim is making friends. You and that other guy and that girl all seem nice. But stay out of my business, all right?"

"I didn't mean to get in your business. I was just curious."

"I mean, this. My business." He circled his finger. "This place. Steer clear."

"OK. Sorry."

"Keep the dough," he said. "It's money for being cool."

It wasn't a big deal to be home an hour late—I could have stayed at school or stopped at Oliver's house—but I still had a long walk in front of me. I hurried past the flashing kangaroo and the Laundromat, crossed First Street, and got to the corner just in time to wait for a train. There was some early rush-hour traffic, too, backed up for half a block or more, belching exhaust fumes into the winter air.

I stood there shivering while the train went by. It was a long one, one after another BNSF car carrying who knows what to who knows where.

And something bounced into my brain like a flashing kangaroo. Ted, the donut scavenger who'd asked Sergei about his brother, was Ted Whaley, the guy at the Laundromat who'd found Dmitri. Heck, I'd *seen* him there. He'd been there the day Oliver and I went to the junkyard.

I might have turned then, run into the Laundromat, and asked Ted what he knew about robots turning on people. But the end of the train was in sight, and I had to get home.

PART III

POLLY

CHAPTER 15

We tried calling our robot Octy, Octobot, Cephalobot, and Rocktopus, but the name that stuck was Polly—short for Polymer. I attached every limb and soldered every connector. Oliver talked me through it, but I was adamant about doing all the work myself.

"I don't see what the big deal is," he said. "I said you can enter it in the mall contest even if we build this together."

"It wouldn't seem fair. Shh. I need to concentrate." I carefully threaded a polymer leg through a hole on an omni-wheel and tightened a nut the size of a squashed pea. The omni-wheel was actually going to be part of the head—it would give the robot the ability to twist around without shuffling its feet.

"Nice work," said Oliver. "You know, I've never seen you like this."

"Seen me like what?"

"Really getting into something. Last year I had to do all the work."

"You wouldn't *let* me help last year," I reminded him.

"You didn't come up with any ideas last year, or read a book, or spend all day figuring things out. If you had, I would have let you."

"Good point." It never occurred to me that he was as frustrated with me for being a deadweight as I was with him for running the show. "Sorry I wasn't much help."

"It's fine," he said. "It's just cool to see what you can do when you're motivated." The way he said it was annoying and loaded with implication.

"It's not what you think," I said. "It's not about Rocky." It wasn't, really. I wanted Polly to win her battle against Rocky and Dmitri's robot, but not to get even. I just wanted to prove myself.

"I was talking about the mall competition and the prize money," he said.

"Oh, right."

The epoxy was dry. I attached another leg, Oliver keeping silent so I could focus.

"Hey," he said when I was done. "Did you ever learn about Rocky and Dmitri's robot?"

"No," I said. I thought about Dmitri. "Let's still assume it's a car."

"Or an otter?" Oliver suggested.

"Right."

"I wish we knew more," he said.

"Well, they don't know anything about ours, so I guess it's fair." What would Rocky think when she saw the octopus? Would she remember the one from the aquarium? Would she know I'd built it for her?

We finished up around midnight. I plugged in the logic controller and turned it on. Polly beeped hello and went for a walk across the living room floor. She stopped at the door.

"She still needs weapons, but she's looking good," said Oliver.

"And a better program," I said. "She doesn't do much right now." I'd taken some simple code from Oliver's robot book and tweaked it to work with the polymer legs. Peter had sent us the instructions.

The door handle turned. I felt a moment of worry that the robot would get whapped, but Polly sensed an object was coming toward her and hurried out of the way.

Oliver's mother came in, saw the thing, and screamed.

"Mom. It's OK. It's a robot."

"I should have known," she said with a relieved smile. "At first it looked like a giant spider. Gorgeous robot. You've outdone yourself."

"It's Jim's," said Oliver.

"Really?"

"Really." He sounded like a proud papa. "Hey, is everything all right? You said you wouldn't be home tonight."

"Well," she said slowly, "Peter proposed . . . and I said no. It kind of ruined the evening."

Oliver blinked. "You said no?" He sounded disappointed but not especially surprised.

"Did you know he was going to pop the question?" she asked.

"I suspected," said Oliver.

His mother sighed. "We can talk in the morning, OK? I could use some sleep."

Oliver had two beds. I picked up a stuffed bear from the extra one.

"Danny," I said. "Long time no see."

"Hello, James," said the bear. Oliver's dad's voice sounded from across the years.

"Want to play animals?" I asked.

"Yes," said the bear. "What does a doggy say?"

"Moo," I answered.

"Are you sure?" said Danny. "What does a doggy say?"

"Oink."

"Are you sure? What does a doggy say?"

"Woof woof."

"Right!" Danny raised his arms like I'd scored a touchdown, then lowered them. One arm stuck halfway up. "And what does a kitty say?"

"No more animals." I put the bear down.

"Come here, Danny," said Oliver. The bear took a few steps and fell over.

"He's seen better days," I said.

"Yeah. I've tried to keep him working, but I guess I was just too hard on him as a kid."

"He's still amazing."

"You can buy toys like this at Babies 'R' Us now," said Oliver.

"Not as good as Danny."

"My dad just made it because he felt guilty for working all the time and not being around. Never occurred to him he could sell it for a gazillion dollars."

"He did make a gazillion dollars, just making a different kind of robot."

"Well. Not quite a gazillion." He picked Danny up and set it on the desk. "Good night, Danny."

"Good night, Junior." The bear sang "Twinkle, Twinkle, Little Star," and I think I fell asleep before the second verse. I woke up before dawn and slipped out of the house. I figured it was best if Oliver and his mom had the morning to themselves.

I went to work as soon as I got home. Ninety minutes later, I sent Celeste rolling into Penny's room.

"Good morning, Penny!" the robot said in a flat voice. The echoes from the tin head made her sound extra robotic and evil. "Wake up. I want to play."

Penny's eyes popped open.

"Good morning, Penny!" Celeste said again. "Wake up. I want to play."

Penny yelped and pulled the covers over her head.

"Good morning, Penny!" Celeste started again.

"Make her shut up!" said Penny.

I picked up the robot and turned off the switch. "It's no big deal," I said.

"That wasn't funny. I've had nightmares about robots lately," she said. She lowered the covers. "How did you do that?"

"I got a text-to-speech device from Oliver."

Penny's eyes turned from cross to conspiratorial. "I have an idea."

She invited Maggie over later that day. Maggie was as much a rival as a friend—she and Penny were always trying to one-up each other. Penny would get a new toy, and Maggie would brag that she had a bigger, better version. Maggie would start reading a thick book, and Penny would get it from the library and race to finish it first.

"Say hello to Maggie, Celeste," Rocky said.

"Hi, Maggie," the robot said.

"Hold up some fingers," Penny told her. "We're teaching Celeste to count."

Maggie held up three fingers.

"How many fingers is she holding up?" Penny asked.

"Three," Celeste answered.

"You got lucky!" said Maggie. "Do it again."

They played several rounds, Celeste getting the answer right every time—even when Maggie held up two fists. "None," Celeste answered. It was possible to program a robot to do that, but we'd cheated. Penny just waved a hand in front of one of the sensors whenever Maggie held up fingers. Celeste counted the times Penny waved her hand.

Jim: Everything all right over there?

Oliver: Yeah. Mom is drinking wine and watching rom-coms.

Jim: Ugh.

Oliver: I dunno what the problem is. She's known P forever. She seems to love him. Why not just marry him?

Jim: Yeah. Nice guy.

Oliver: And he's loaded. ☺

Jim: You disappointed?

Oliver: Me?

Jim: I dunno. Just wondering. You know, new dad. All that.

Oliver: Wanted it when I was 8-10. Now just want Mom to be happy.

Jim: Sure.

Oliver: Srsly.

Jim: OK. Just wondering.

Oliver: Mom wants me to go watch movie with her. Ttyl.

Jim: Hope it's nothing too bad.

Oliver: Hugh Grant is in it. I'll bring my barf bag.

Jim: LOL.

Oliver: When the Whitney Houston CDs come out, I'm moving in with you.
Jim: LOL x 2.

Penny and I spent the next week in a sea of curly brackets and parentheses, programming Polly to sense if an enemy was approaching and to know when her opponent was exposed. I would type up the code while Penny read aloud from the book. She was pretty smart, figuring out stuff right along with me.

What slowed us down was computer time. We could only use the office when Mom and Dad weren't in there, which was frustrating. I really needed my own computer.

"Is this supposed to be the octopus from the aquarium?" Penny asked the first time she saw the new robot.

"Yeah." I was glad she recognized it.

"Did you show it to Rocky yet?"

"Not yet," I told her. "Why?"

"Because. I just wondered."

She was on to me. I went with the octopus as a message to Rocky. What exactly the message was, I wasn't sure.

"It's cool," said Penny.

"Thanks. Let's see if it works."

We plugged in the logic controller so we could test our program.

In a few days, Polly and Celeste could play tag or hide-and-seek. They could even "talk" by flashing colored lights at each other. Polly would flash a random color, Celeste would sense it and flash back the same color.

"We need to test them in a mock battle," I suggested.

"Nuh-uh," said Penny. "I don't want Celeste to beat up Polly."

I laughed. Celeste didn't have any weapons.

"Nobody will hurt anybody," I told her.

"All right, but I get to stop the fight at any time," she said.

We cleared a space on the kitchen floor and let them at it. We decided the first robot to tag the other one three times was the winner. Polly could use any of her eight legs to tag Celeste, and Celeste could use any part of her cardboard frame to tag Polly.

The first round went beautifully, Polly dropping and letting Celeste roll over her, just as I'd planned. I'd disabled the jump feature so she wouldn't send Celeste flying, but the second the cardboard robot was past, Polly reached out and tagged her.

Celeste turned back and Polly dropped again. This time Celeste stopped midway and rolled back the way she'd came. Polly was confused, hopping up and reaching forward while Celeste tagged her from behind.

"Score!" Penny shouted.

"She's not supposed to change directions!" I said.

"I made some changes," said Penny. "I wanted it to be fair."

I remembered what Rolf said about adapting to what the

programmer didn't expect. If Polly had been programmed that way, she'd figure out Celeste's trick and change her own behavior. But she couldn't, and Celeste won the contest three to one.

The boxy robot raised her wire arms in victory.

"What the—she can't do that!" I said.

"I've been making all kinds of changes," said Penny.

The science fair was on Wednesday. We had the regular part of the fair first, where people could come by and see the robot and ask questions. Oliver had thrown together the poster and report—our hypothesis was something about the new-era robot parts.

"Where did you get these?" one of the judges asked, squinting at the polymer legs.

"An old colleague of my dad's," Oliver admitted.

"Hmm. Well, it's certainly remarkable," the judge said. I had a feeling we'd just lost points for having an inside connection, but I didn't care if we won the science fair. I was only interested in the battle at the end of it. I wanted to see how Polly would do in a competition, and even more than that, I wanted to see Rocky's face when she saw Polly.

Our display was popular, and neither of us was able to sneak away and see Dmitri and Rocky's robot. We didn't get a chance until the contest. We'd guessed correctly—it was something between an otter and a car. The front two-thirds of a model car had been hinged to the back two-thirds of another, making a stretch limo that could gyrate. The robot's head had a snapping hood-mouth with nails for teeth; the tail had a peaked fin swinging a tiny wrecking ball. It looked more like an alligator than an otter, but I knew what they were going for.

When Rocky saw the octopus, I didn't see even a flicker of recognition in her eyes. She had a good poker face.

We used a corner of the gym for the contest, with no official ring or borders. A kid used an app on his phone as the timer. It rang like a boxing bell, and the match was under way.

The alligator came at our octopus and proved to be quicker and more agile than it looked, twisting wildly, the jaw chomping and gnashing, the tail swinging threateningly. It was a cool robot, but it wasn't well programmed. They'd just pointed it in the right direction and hoped for the best.

The match didn't last long. Polly sensed a danger was coming and collapsed. The gator started to roll over her and triggered a sensor on her head. She kicked up and skittered away, sending the other robot tumbling. It landed on its back and kicked, helpless as a turtle. The crowd clapped a little, but I could tell they were disappointed. They wanted more of a fight.

Polly decided it was safe and crept closer to finish the job. This was the toughest part of the program, for me—knowing when the opponent was helpless. Polly could track the other robot and know when it wasn't moving, but she would be in trouble if it was playing possum. I'd need to improve that before the next competition.

Since Polly was a lightweight robot, she couldn't really pack a punch. Her only real weapon was herself, leaping up and tossing her opponent like a sumo wrestler. Practically everything I could think of as a weapon was against the rules—flame, projectiles, electric charges, or globs of glue. But Oliver's mom had given me an idea. Polly ran circles around the gator, spraying loops and whorls of fishing line. The gator did get one good lick in, a random swing of its spiked tail catching one of Polly's legs. There was a raucous hooray from the crowd, who were thirsty for more action, but a moment later the gator was wrapped up like a housefly.

"I think that's a match," said Mr. Cole.

"Lame battle," said one of the spectators as the small crowd wandered off.

Dmitri carefully disentangled his robot while Rocky looked on.

"Cool otter," I told her.

"You knew it wasn't an alligator," she said softly. "We named it Viddy. It's the Russian word for *otter*." She then took an icicle and stabbed me in the heart.

"Oliver's spider is beautiful," she said.

CHAPTER 16

"It's all political correctness," Oliver complained. The winning science-fair projects had to do with pollution, assistive technology, and solar power.

"You mean they favored positive applications of science?" Rocky asked.

"Exactly," he said.

We were at Sidney's on Saturday afternoon. We were the first ones there, and Sid was still busy getting things set up. He finally noticed us and came over.

"What can I get you guys today?" He pushed his paper hat back, ready with his pencil and notepad.

"DangeRoo," I said. The burger stuffed with cream cheese and jalapeños.

"One Roo. Livin' on the edge," said Sid.

"Pig in a Pocket," said Dmitri. The one stuffed with bacon and cheddar.

"Sidney's classic," said Oliver.

"Roo, Pig, and a Sid. What about the lady?"

Rocky was staring hopelessly at the menu. "Don't you have a veggie burger?"

"You want a burger stuffed with veggies?" Sid asked, his face puzzled.

"No, I mean a vegetarian patty."

"I've heard rumors there's such a thing, but not here. How about Swiss cheese, mushrooms, peppers, and onions on a bun?"

"That sounds pretty good," she said.

"One Supersid, no pocket," he said, heading back to the kitchen.

"So tell me about your robot," said Dmitri. "Where did you get the legs? I searched all the robot suppliers on the Web and couldn't find anything like them."

"We've got a source," said Oliver.

"Lucky you," said Dmitri. "Can I buy some supplies from your secret source?"

"Whoa, whoa, I didn't hear that!" Sid said, returning with our Cokes.

"It's nothing illegal," I told him. "We're talking about robots."

"Oh man. You know there used to be a robot factory down the road?"

"Yeah. We know," said Oliver. "My dad used to work there."

"Oh." Sid saw Oliver's grave face. "Sad story. I'll go make your burgers." He split again.

"Secret parts or not, your robot was really cool," said Dmitri.

"Your robot was pretty neat, too," said Oliver. "We

should have taken first and second place. Nobody cares about pollution or solar power."

"I do," said Rocky.

"Well, fine," said Oliver. "In the bigger sense, so do I. But those projects didn't do anything new."

"I don't see how it makes a difference," said Dmitri. "All you get for winning is a ribbon, anyway."

"But the winner goes on to district," said Oliver. "And the winners from there can go on to a national competition. Some of them get scholarships and sponsorships. It can be worth tens of thousands of dollars."

"OK, but I don't see those prizes going to toy robots," said Dmitri.

"You're right." Oliver fumed. "But some of us aren't in it for the money." Dmitri didn't know how much those honors meant to Oliver.

"Well, *I'm* in it for the money," said Dmitri. He pulled a folded piece of paper out of his pocket and handed it to us. "And I want a rematch."

Oliver glanced at it. It was a flyer for the robot competition at the mall. "We're already entering," he said. "Jim's entering this year's robot, and I'm entering last year's robot. With some modifications, of course."

"Oh. Well, I just found out about it. I wonder if Viddy has a chance?" He started to fold it up again.

"Wait," I said. I took the flyer back. Dmitri had an updated version. "Check out the bottom line," I told Oliver.

He read it aloud: "'Featuring special guest judge, robotics expert Peter Clayton.' Hmm. Small world."

"What?" Rocky asked.

"We kind of know the judge," I whispered. "Oliver's mom recently dumped him."

"Seriously?" Rocky asked. "Will he hold it against you?"

"He'll be objective," said Oliver. He pointed at me. "You're the one that has to worry. He knows Polly has high-end parts from a secret source." He stopped short of telling them Peter *was* the secret source.

Sid arrived with our orders. Dmitri tore into his burger. "This is really good," he said. "I never knew about this place."

"I saw the sign a million times but never came in," said Rocky.

"My mom says my dad used to eat here all the time, back when he worked at Nomicon," said Oliver. He looked up at Sid. "Did you know him?"

"I was still in high school when that place closed. But I remember how funny it was when the science geeks came in. They looked kind of out of place with the grease monkeys and construction workers."

"How long has this place been here?" asked Rocky, walking right into Sid's trap. He gave her the whole since-1955 story, telling us that the original Sid, his granddad, ran the place for twenty-odd years, and his own dad ran it for another twenty.

"That kangaroo was my idea." He pointed at the

neon sign. "When Dad took over, he tried to modernize the place and wanted a new sign. I guess I was learning about Australia at the time, because I came up with that. Sydney is the biggest city in Australia. They have kangaroos, and kangaroos have pockets. I was pretty proud of myself."

"Hey, we saw the original sign!" she told him.

"No kidding?" Sid looked skeptical. "Dad got rid of all that stuff years ago. He was tired of it taking up space in the storeroom."

"It's just down the road," she said. "There's a junkyard there."

I shot her a look. She seemed confused, but got that she should quit talking.

"The place is all locked up," I said. "Barbed-wire fence. No trespassing signs."

"Ah well. Would've been cool to get it back." Sid returned to the kitchen.

"So, about these robot battles," Dmitri said to Oliver. "Do you think we'd stand a chance?"

"Not against me," said Oliver frankly. "And Jim's robot already beat you."

"What's third place?"

"I think it's a gift card to Lego."

"Alex would love that," he said. "I'm in."

"Don't I get to do anything?" Penny asked.

"Huh?" I was on the computer, updating Polly's program.

"This is supposed to be *our* robot, but you've done *everything.*"

"That's not true. You've helped a lot."

"Not lately."

I sighed. "Do you think you can work on the program?" The code had grown a lot more complex since we'd started.

"I programmed Celeste to beat Polly," she reminded me.

"Fine." I needed to work on the robot itself, anyway—giving Polly weapons. I explained what I wanted, a feint attack and retreat that would test if other robots were really vulnerable or playing possum.

"Just copy this code and change this line," I explained.

"I got it, I got it," she said. She sat down.

"Will we be able to beat Oliver's robot?" she asked.

"I don't know," I said.

"It's going to be really fast and really strong and really smart," she said.

"I know, but maybe its strengths will be its weakness," I said.

"What does that mean?"

"I don't know. I heard it in a kung-fu movie." I went to arm our octopus.

Mom gave Penny and me a ride to the mall on the day of the tournament. Penny was wearing a gaudy plastic rainbow bracelet with a dangling pink heart.

"What's that for?" Mom asked.

"It's my good-luck charm," said Penny. "Not that we need it, because we have the best robot."

"Well, it's been really great to see you kids working together on something," said Mom. "Even if I don't understand what this is all about."

"It's fun, too," said Penny.

"Yeah," I agreed. It *was* fun, but I was still focused on winning the prize money.

The competition was in a big atrium in the east hallway. There was a stage and circular seating like a theater, with plenty more room for people to stand and watch the show. The place was packed when we got there. There were over twenty entries for the younger kids using remote-controlled robots, and the older kids had almost forty entries. There were only eight contestants entered in the autonomous category. I felt pretty good until I saw the lineup posted on the wall.

1. Lori Elsworth & Katie Kirkland
2. Rochelle Blankenship & Dmitri Volkov
3. Oliver Newton
4. Alan Janz
5. James & Penelope Knox
6. Timothy McCaughey
7. Nelson Varona
8. Rolf Strauss

I tapped the last name on the list. "I met this guy. He makes Oliver look like a dunce."

"Nobody makes Oliver look like a dunce," said Rocky.

"He makes Oliver *feel* like a dunce, then," I whispered. I wondered why he even entered. He was probably in it for the glory, same as Oliver.

"He has to play by the same rules as the rest of us," said Dmitri.

"I'm just saying. His robot is going to be amazing."

We saw Oliver across the ring, making some last-minute adjustments to his robot. Particularly scary were Robbie's new arms, which were long and stout, and had fists the size of oilcans. I went over to talk to him.

"Hey," I said. "Did you notice who entered?"

"Nope."

I pointed out Rolf, who was carrying a black case and looked supremely confident. Oliver's eyes widened.

"How is that fair? He's in with the judge."

"So are we. In theory."

"Never mind," he said. "Peter will be fair."

"Still doesn't seem right," I said. "Rolf is out of our league."

"Speak for yourself. I'm glad he's in this." Oliver lubricated Robbie's joints, patted him on the head, and picked him up. "He's been teaching robots the alphabet, while I've been building robots that destroy other robots."

CHAPTER 17

The first bout was between Rolf's robot and the two-girl team. Their robot was the basic metal humanoid, with magnets for hands.

"Why magnets?" Penny asked.

"To pull the other robots down."

"What if the other robot isn't made of metal?"

"Then that thing's in trouble."

It *was* in trouble. Rolf's robot was a hulking egg-shaped mystery of hard plastic. The magnetic robot did a quick scan, spotted its opponent, and moved in. A saw came out of its torso, the hands reached for the hard shell of the egg, and—and nothing. The magnets couldn't attach themselves.

The egg opened at the top, spreading its shell into four pieces. They lowered until they became helicopter blades and started spinning. The magnet robot backed away. The egg lifted into the air and chased after it, catching it with its blades. The blades weren't made of metal, but they were strong and sharp, digging a deep gouge into the other robot's midsection.

Mom covered her face as if it were a living thing.

"Stop!" One of the girls leaped into the ring and rescued their robot. It meant immediate disqualification, but they would have lost anyway.

"It's OK," Penny whispered.

Mom uncovered her eyes and saw that it was over.

"When does your turn come?"

"I think we're last in this round."

"I won't be able to watch," she said. "You put all that work into your robot. It would be a shame to see it get hurt."

"It's OK, really. It's what it's made for." I was putting a brave face on it, but it killed me to think of Rolf's robot turning our octopus into something you'd order at a Japanese restaurant.

"They should have a competition for robots that actually do things," said Mom.

"They do," I told her. But the amount of functions that would go into folding laundry or washing dishes boggled my brain.

Oliver's match was against Timothy, who had an R2-D2–style robot with an assortment of weapons. The R2 clone didn't manage to use any of them before Oliver's robot sped in and flattened it.

Viddy had a tougher battle, against a similar vehicle-robot that hurled tethered weights at its opponent. Viddy took a few dents, but once its chomping teeth bit through the tether wires, the other robot was defenseless.

Polly's first match was against a guy named Nelson who hadn't shown up. It was an automatic forfeit, so we advanced.

"Hooray!" Penny jumped up and down.

"It's no fair," said one of the girls who'd been defeated by Rolf's egg.

"Sorry," said Peter. "Those are the rules."

They gave us a break before the next round to make any necessary repairs. In the meantime, the other robot contests were under way—eight- to twelve-year-olds with remote-controlled bots made from kits.

Mom bought us lunch at Bubba Gump's. It was one of my favorite restaurants, but I couldn't eat.

"Nervous?" Mom asked.

"A little."

"Not me," said Penny. "We have the smartest robot. Can I have your shrimp?"

We got lucky on the draw for the second round. Polly would have a rematch with Viddy, whom she'd already beaten. But first Robbie was going to take on that flying egg. The crowd hushed when Oliver and Rolf entered the ring. Everyone knew they were the two best in the competition, but also that Rolf's robot was in a whole other league, stunning and mysterious, a piece of technology from the future. I knew that whatever happened, Oliver would let the battle proceed. We would see what else that egg could do.

The round began much as the first one had—Robbie went on attack while the egg thing bided its time, even taking a few punches until Robbie was off balance and tottering. The egg opened fast this time, its helicopter blade whirring loudly. Robbie lurched forward and landed a punch right on the flashing yolk at the center. The egg scooted aside, apparently unhurt, then went to work on Robbie's feet from behind. Robbie turned and landed a cudgel on one of the blades.

The egg flipped, skidding toward the crowd. People hastened out of the way, but the egg got its bearings before it left the ring. Robbie tried to march after it, but the egg had cut his actuators—the cords between the brain and the legs. He just stood there.

If a robot can look panicked, Robbie sure did. The egg returned. Robbie turned at the waist to greet it, but was too slow, and the blade bit into his arm. After that it was like seeing the sharks eat their chum at the aquarium. The egg darted back and forth, neatly cutting all the wires until Robbie's sensors were dull, his actuators inoperable. Oliver's face was expressionless as his best robot was turned into scrap metal.

"I sure hope Polly wins," he whispered to me. "Or the gator. Just not that thing."

I started to get Polly ready for the next fight, when I saw Dmitri and Rocky talking to Peter. He tried to argue with them, but Dmitri was insistent.

"What's going on?" Mom asked.

"I don't know," I said.

"I'm afraid that team number two has withdrawn from the competition," Peter announced.

The crowd buzzed. Why would Dmitri and Rocky quit? They retreated into the crowd. I'd have to get an explanation later.

"This is so bogus!" the same girl from earlier complained. "That stupid spider is in the finals and it hasn't even had to fight yet!"

"No fair!" the other girl said, starting a slow clap. A few other people joined in, but the protest didn't last long. I felt sick to my stomach. If we lost, would we still get second place, even without winning a single contest?

"If both contestants are ready, we can proceed to the next round," said Peter. He looked at Rolf, who nodded. He didn't look at me. He knew Polly was ready, because she hadn't even been in a fight yet today.

Rolf stepped forward to shake my hand, then shook Penny's. "Your spider robot looks awesome," he said.

"Thanks. Don't be mad when it makes your egg into an omelet," she said.

"Aha. Rivalry," he said, as if he was observing something from a distance and barely recognized it.

The buzzer sounded to start the round. The egg waited for Polly to make the first move. Since Polly was programmed to do the same thing, there was a long, tense silence.

"Is either of them going to do anything?" someone in the crowd asked.

Another thirty seconds passed. It felt like longer. Penny scanned the crowd, maybe looking for a judge to tell us what to do. She saw somebody she knew and waved. I turned to see who it was.

The crowd started cheering. Polly was on the move! The robot took a tentative step, then another, creeping toward the egg. She lifted a leg and tapped the shell of the egg, then gave it a poke. I'd attached razor-sharp points to her two front legs. The blade slid on the egg's hard surface.

Shocked into action, the egg went into the spin-and-lift mode. Polly halted. I prayed that her sensors would detect an airborne enemy, and they must have, because she dropped. The egg lowered and hummed around her in circles like a confused bee, looking for something to sting.

Polly leaped up at just the right time, her metal head catching a blade of the flying egg and sending the whole thing somersaulting. The crowd gasped as it dipped, one blade scraping the floor. Polly ran after it, spurting her fishing line, entangling the egg's wings.

A hand settled on my shoulder. I looked up and saw Peter.

"Amazing work," he whispered. "Very impressive." He sounded weirdly somber.

I gulped. Was he upset that we'd used the polymer legs?

It looked like Rolf had also used some high-end materials you couldn't buy at the hobby store.

A roar from the crowd got my attention back on the battle. Rolf's egg had regained its bearings, shaken off the lines, and was now hurling toward Polly at lightning speed. Polly didn't drop—the egg was too high to trigger her sensors. It dipped suddenly, and should have taken off enough of her legs to win the battle, but Polly dropped just in time. The underside of her bowl-shaped head caught the wing and sent the flying egg askew again.

Polly popped up and riddled the dead center of the egg with pokes of her razor-tipped front legs. One of her feet got stuck. The egg skipped along the floor, dragging Polly with it. By the time it got loose, both robots were badly damaged.

The buzzer sounded. Peter conferred with a couple of other officials, then came back to Penny and me.

"We need to talk," he said.

He led us away from the rotunda into a side hallway, stopping by the restrooms. I had an uneasy feeling he wasn't about to congratulate us as the winners.

We stopped by a door that read STAFF ONLY, where fewer people were streaming by.

"Did you have any remote controls for your robot, of any kind?" Peter asked me.

"No," I answered. I looked to Penny, who was pursing her lips and looked ready to burst. "Penny?"

"I didn't do anything wrong!" she wailed.

"Are you sure?" Peter asked.

"All I did was wave," she said. "I didn't use a remote control."

The truth hit me. Penny had rigged the sensors the same way she did with Celeste. I'd seen Penny wave just before Polly went into action. I wasn't looking at Penny when our robot had made two or three last-minute moves that saved her neck, but I guessed she'd done it then, too.

Penny held up her left hand, the one with the bracelet. "I had to catch just the right sensor with this. One wave for collapse. Two for jump back up."

"Thanks for your honesty," Peter told Penny. He looked at me. "I'm really disappointed in both of you."

"I didn't know," I said weakly. "It was Penny's idea. She didn't even tell me."

"Don't make it worse by scapegoating your little sister," he said.

"I'm not trying to scapegoat anyone."

"It was my idea!" Penny protested. "I didn't even tell Jim. Honest."

"I know that you kids look out for each other. It's almost sweet. Almost. But I'll have to eliminate your robot from the competition and disqualify you from ever competing again."

"I wasn't going to enter again, anyway. I only even entered to pay you back," I told him.

"You don't owe it to *me* to cheat other kids out of the money. Kids who really labored on their projects."

"We worked really hard on our project, too." He had to kick us out of the competition. I understood that. But I wanted him to see that I'd made a real robot, one that could have beaten any other kid in the competition but his genius protégé. "Check the code. It works."

"Sure it does," he said. He started back to the rotunda. Penny looked at me with wide, uncomprehending eyes.

"Go find Mom," I told her. I didn't want to go back to the competition. I didn't want to hear Peter's announcement. I didn't want to face Oliver or Rocky or Dmitri. I didn't want to face the two girls who already had it in for me.

I didn't want to go home, either. What I really wanted to do was go to the aquarium and leap into the shark tank.

"We have to go back." Penny tugged on my hand.

"We're disqualified."

"I know, but we have to get Polly. She's our robot."

Mom found us. She was carrying the robot.

"The man back there said you were out of the competition?"

"Yeah. Something like that. Can we go?"

"I'm so sorry," said Mom. "I know how hard you two worked on this. It must be a misunderstanding." She tried to hug me, but I wasn't feeling very huggy just then.

* * *

I was lying in bed on Sunday evening, feeling sorry for myself, when Celeste rolled in.

"Knock knock," she said. She pronounced the Ks: "Kanock kanock."

"Who's there?"

"Robot."

"Robot who?"

"Robot nothing. Robots don't have last names," she said. "Ha ha. Ha ha." The robot didn't actually laugh. It said "ha ha, ha ha" in its flat, emotionless voice, which made it sound sarcastic.

"That's terrible, Pen—Celeste."

"Kanock kanock," she repeated.

"No, not again."

"Ro- ro- ro-," she stuttered.

"What, are you broken?"

"Ro- ro- ro- your bot, gently down the stream," said the robot. "Ha ha. Ha ha."

"That doesn't even make sense."

"Kanock kanock."

"Please stop."

"Bot."

I sighed. "Bot who?"

"Bot you can't wait to hear another kanock-kanock joke. Ha ha. Ha ha." That robot thought she was hilarious.

Penny peeked in. "Sorry. I didn't have time to make better jokes. I wanted to cheer you up."

“You did. Thanks.” It was the first useful robot I’d seen that weekend. What would Rolf’s egg do against an all-out assault of knock-knock jokes? I wondered. Crack up, of course. I laughed out loud, and that made Penny join in, even though she didn’t know why I was laughing.

CHAPTER 18

Rocky wasn't at the bus stop Monday morning, which was for the best. I sat by myself, way up front, staring out the window so I didn't have to make eye contact with Oliver when he boarded. I knew he saw me, but he didn't say a word as he passed.

The bus was held up on Victory Drive, stuck in a long, slow-moving chain of cars that stretched back eight or nine blocks. Several kids stood up to get a better look, and the driver shouted at them to sit down again. The bus lurched forward a car length or two at a time.

As we got to First Street, we could see black-and-white police cars, a row of orange cones, and a single officer waving all of the traffic heading north on First Street onto the parkway. That was what was causing the slowdown. Through the treeless corner of the park we could see around the barricade to First Street. The sidewalk in front of Sidney's was littered with shattered glass, the windows covered with cardboard and yellow police tape. I felt a chill go through me.

"Somebody shot up the Kangaroo Burger!" a kid shouted.

"It looks like another tornado ripped through!" another kid added.

The bus finally turned onto First Street, putting the scene behind us.

By the time we got to school, the restaurant was already forgotten. There were shootings and break-ins all the time in North Minneapolis, and for most kids, this was just more of the same. I got online during lunch and checked all the local news sites, but none of them had the story. Maybe broken windows in North Minneapolis weren't newsworthy.

School was lonely. Oliver ignored me, and Rocky and Dmitri were in a little world of each other.

I tried to talk to Oliver on the bus ride home. He was in a seat by himself.

"Do you want to go check on Sid?"

He didn't answer, and he didn't move his bag so I could sit down.

"Really?" I asked him. "You're going to be like this?"

He didn't say anything, which I took as a yes. He was going to be like that. I sat a few seats behind him, watching the slushy streets through the window. Maybe Oliver had a right to be mad, but that was just a competition. This was serious.

I found Sid behind the restaurant, smoking a cigarette. He saw me, sucked in his breath, and exhaled plumes of smoke that were as dense as clouds in the cold air. "It's you," he said.

"What happened?"

"I don't even know." He took another draw on his cigarette and coughed. "Or I do know, but if I told anyone, I'd be put right into a rubber room."

I remembered the original sign for Sidney's and had a hunch. "Did you go to the junkyard? The one on Half Street?"

"Hey, you seem to know something about this," he said.

"Practically nothing," I admitted. "I've heard things, is all."

"I was here really early this morning and decided to go take a look. Man, that place is freaky. It's like the elephants' graveyard for appliances. Anyway, I saw the sign, right by the fence. I went in, slid it out under the gate, and brought it back here. Thought I'd hang it on the wall, then call Dad and tell him to bring Grandpa for lunch. I'd surprise 'em both. But before I even got the drill, I glanced up and out the window and saw—"

He stopped to drag on his cigarette. "This is the part you won't believe." He let loose with a cloud of cigarette smoke.

"I believe in lots of crazy stuff," I told him.

"OK. I saw this thing. It looked like something a kid made from an Erector set, zipping across the street toward me."

"A robot," I said.

"Like a cross between a robot and a dinosaur," he said.

"A robot dinosaur," I echoed. Penny said the robot she'd

seen at Nomicon—the robot that didn't exist—looked "lizardy."

"I thought it was a pretty cool gizmo until it shot up my place and jumped in the window," said Sid. "It aimed its beak at me and started clicking and squeaking at me. I thought, Is this the new thing, people committing robberies with robots? I started emptying the cash register, but the thing flashed its light at the old sign. So, I grabbed the thing and hauled it back. I didn't even bother with my jacket and gloves. Look at my hands." He held them up so I could see the red creases slashing across his fingers. "I slid the sign back under the fence and said no hard feelings and the thing left me alone." He tossed his cigarette into a mound of snow by the Dumpster. "Why does it care about an old sign?"

"I don't know," I said.

"But you believe me?"

"Yeah. Sure. You don't seem crazy." Penny had seen something, and so had the guy at the Laundromat. Then there was Dmitri, who'd been tased and left for dead. Maybe he'd seen more than he admitted.

"Well, I guess I'll stay away from now on," said Sid. "Plus quit smoking again. First pack I've bought in six years." He dropped the cigarette into a pile of snow and immediately lit another.

When I got home, I searched the top of my dresser and found a Post-it note with a phone number scribbled on it. I dialed the number, halfway hoping for voice mail, but the woman answered.

On TV, cops always answer with their last name: "Walsh!" but she answered like a customer-service person. "You've called the fourth precinct detective line; this is Officer Walsh. How may I assist you?"

"This is Jim Knox," I told her. "We talked about Dmitri Volkov? The missing teenager who isn't missing anymore?"

"Sure, sure," she said. I heard computer keys clacking and knew she was looking it up and refreshing her memory. "He was released from the hospital and seems to be doing fine. Do you have any additional information you'd like to share?"

"Well, yeah. That's why I called." I decided I couldn't come right out with robot dinosaurs firing ray guns. If I could get the police there, they would see them for themselves. "I know that it happened on the site of the old Nomicon campus. There's a bunch of junk there, somebody seems to be living there. Hoboes, maybe." I gritted my teeth. Hoboes? Where did I come up with that?

"Sir, the former Nomicon site is considered a hazardous area. It's fenced off for a reason. Did you breach the fence and trespass?"

"Sort of."

"Well, don't let it happen again," she said.

"But there's somebody *there*. Somebody dangerous. They busted the windows at Sidney's Diner. . . ."

"I'll add these notes to the report," she said. "You, stay clear of the area." She hung up.

I knew it. If I was going to get the police there, I had to come up with something better than hoboes breaking windows. I went to my sock drawer and dug out the roll of bills Sergei had given me. There was just enough to fund my terrible idea that would probably get me killed.

I needed to skip school. Since Mom and Dad both worked from home, I couldn't fake sickness and split the moment they left, like a lot of kids could. I didn't think I could go to school first and slip away without being seen, either. I needed somebody who knew how to pull it off, somebody who'd probably done it before. So I sent Dmitri a message. We hadn't spoken since the robot competition, but if anyone could forgive me for cheating, it would have to be him.

Jim: Did you ever skip school?

Dmitri: What makes you think that?

Jim: Ur gone a lot. That's all.

Dmitri: Sometimes Alex has a bad day & he can't be home alone. Mom works. Dad works. Sergei works. Masha's having a hard time at school, so they ask me.

Jim: Oh.

Dmitri: If u do want to skip, just do it. Policy is they only call ur parents after 3 absences.

Jim: Srsly?

Dmitri: Says so right in the manual. U should read it.

Jim: So you can skip school 3 times w/no problem?

Dmitri: Twice. 3rd time they call.

Jim: Right. But we get 2 free days. Amazing. I owe u 1.

Dmitri: Know how to pay me back?

Jim: How?

Dmitri: Whatever ur up to, I want in.

Jim: It's dangerous & might get us both killed.

Dmitri: Even better.

On Tuesday morning I left home like I was catching the school bus, went around the corner, and hopped on a city bus headed downtown. I got off at Nicollet Avenue and went to the Barnes & Noble coffee shop. Dmitri was already there, reading a newspaper and drinking a cup of tea and looking forty years old.

"What now?" he asked.

"There's a Target across the street," I told him. "It opens at eight." In addition to Target Field, the Target Center, and the Target corporate headquarters, there was an actual Target store in downtown Minneapolis.

We had a few minutes to kill. I explained what happened at the robot competition.

"I just wish we hadn't dropped out," he said. "Rocky said you needed the money, and that neither of us would beat that other guy if we fought each other first."

"You didn't have to do that," I said. "But thanks."

"It's done," he said. "That egg would have won anyway." He checked a clock on the wall. "Two minutes to. Let's go."

We crossed the street, went into the store, and headed straight for the electronics department.

The clerk raised his eyebrow when I paid for a video camera in cash.

"Birthday money," I said, even though he hadn't asked.

"We're going to make a zombie movie," Dmitri added. "Do you have fake blood?"

"Only during Halloween season," he said. "There's a costume shop a few blocks west of here."

"Thanks. That's very helpful. Hey, do you want to be in the movie? We need extras. You just need to stagger around and drool."

"I get plenty of practice working here, but I'll pass." He gave me my change. I could feel him rolling his eyes at us as we left the store.

We got on the bus, heading back north. I took the camera out of the box and put in a tape and the battery. It came with a rechargeable battery pack, and I was glad to see it had an initial charge.

"It's a nice camera," said Dmitri. "Can I see?" He reached out for it.

"I'll hold on to my cameras around you," I said.

"I guess I deserve that," he said.

"Hey, I was just kidding." I let him take the camera. He peered at me through the viewer.

"I never stole anything before that," he told me. "I just wanted to prove I could."

"To Sergei?"

"Yeah, he's always saying I'm such a goody-goody."

"He doesn't mean it as an insult," I told him. "He's proud of you."

"Maybe so, but it comes off like he knows so much more about the world, just because he's been to jail."

"He's been to jail?" I pretended to be surprised. I knew he was on probation.

"Three months," said Dmitri. "He stole a car."

"Wow."

"It's where he first got to work on cars," said Dmitri, "so I guess it was a good experience."

Was Sergei still a car thief? I wondered. What would he do to me if I told anyone about that Audi in his backyard?

We came to our stop. I filled my backpack with camera cables and instructions and left the box on the bus. We walked through the park, past the usual businesses.

"This is where you hid?" I asked as we passed the Laundromat.

"I don't remember it well," he admitted. "My memory's hazy, after the attack."

Sidney's had new panes of glass in front, but no kangaroo. I missed the kangaroo. We marched down the road to Half Street.

CHAPTER 19

The sun glared from across the river, melting the snow, making the usual crawl space wet and slushy. I slung my backpack on the fence and went through first, wetting my knees and elbows. Dmitri passed me the camera and came through himself. He was bigger, and it was a tighter squeeze.

Rivulets of water ran every which way, meeting up to form tiny rivers and ponds. Slippery ones—Dmitri found himself doing a two-step, landed on his bottom.

"It's treacherous," he said.

"Seriously." I helped him up, and we walked slowly down the winding path to the riverbank.

"So let me ask you something," I said. "When you were here before, did you see anything? Something you didn't tell anyone about?"

"Like what?" he said. He looked at me intently. He wants me to say it first, I realized.

"I haven't seen anything myself," I admitted. "But Sid at the restaurant says he saw a kind of—robot dinosaur? And my sister said something similar. She saw something that's still giving her nightmares."

"I don't know what I saw," said Dmitri. "A flash of something, then I got tased. But I see them in my sleep. Didn't know if it was a memory or just a nightmare."

"I wonder why they only go on attack some of the time," I said. "I've been here four times now and haven't even seen one. The one time a robot zapped at me, I didn't even go past the fence."

"I don't know," said Dmitri. "Maybe sometimes they're asleep."

"Yeah, right." Robots didn't need to sleep.

"Let's go down to the buildings."

"All right."

We headed down the path, Dmitri's limp more noticeable as he tried to keep up. We stopped at the front of the crumbling building that used to be Nomicon. There was no junk here. People had spared the ruins, either out of respect or because it was too far to go.

The metal doors were locked, but a corner of the building had disintegrated. Dmitri leaped over the crumbled cement. I started to set the camera down so I could climb in.

"Don't put it down," said Dmitri. He reached out to take the camera.

"What?"

"I have a theory," he said. He held the camera while I climbed in. We were in a sloped, skewed hallway.

"This isn't safe." Dmitri hopped a couple of times, making the floor vibrate.

"Yeah, especially when you do that."

He stopped.

I started the camera and left it rolling, scanning the hallway.

"The explosion must have been downstairs." I swung open a fire door, guessing there was a stairwell. There was, but it was pitch black.

"We should have brought a flashlight," he said.

"The camera has one." I turned it on. It was pretty pathetic, a tiny beam of light that only went about twenty-five feet, but it was better than nothing. I wondered how much life the camera battery had.

"So people died here?" Dmitri asked.

"Oliver's dad did."

"Wow. I did not know that."

"Now you know."

The fire door at the bottom of the stairs was blown off the hinges. We walked across debris into a big, charred room with the twisted shells of computer towers, caved-in monitors, and melted glass spilled across the floor. The desks and chairs had been reduced to ashes.

I stooped to pick up a lump of smoky glass in the shape of a tear. It was peculiar and beautiful, something ordinary transformed by the effects of extreme physics.

"They never cleaned this place up," said Dmitri. "I wonder why not?"

"I don't know." I realized that Oliver's dad must have

died in this room. I turned off the camera. The presence of death and destruction overwhelmed me.

"I need to get out of here," he said.

"Me too. Let's go."

We walked slowly, like cars in a funeral procession, up the steps and down the creaking hallway. I heard a cracking sound behind me and felt a sudden surge of panic: I needed to get out of that place, and *now*. I sprinted down the hall, feeling the floor shudder with every step, and climbed through the hole so quickly I ripped a hole in my pants on the ragged cement.

Dmitri was right behind me, but climbed out more slowly. I helped pull him out into the sunshine.

"Everything all right?" he asked.

"Yeah," I said. "Just got the willies, I guess." I'd probably just heard Dmitri's heavy boots on the floor behind me. I took a few deep breaths, tried to slow my heartbeat by sheer will.

"You could have made the floor collapse," he said.

"Sorry."

"It's all good," he said. "Let's go."

We started back up the zigzag path to the embankment. When I reached the first bend, I realized Dmitri wasn't with me. I couldn't even see him.

"Dmitri?"

There was no answer. My heart pounded. Had they gotten him?

"DMITRI!"

"Here!" a calm voice shouted back, from way off to the right. I saw Dmitri's flat boot prints veering off the trail, and there he was—behind some bushes, using his arm to sweep the snow off a lime-green hulk of an old car. The car was half buried in snow, tangled up with weeds and sprouting trees.

"It's a Superbird!" he shouted. "Get this on video!"

Seriously? Suddenly we were just looking at cars?

"I want to show this to Sergei," he explained.

"Fine." I turned on the camera and zoomed in on the car. I started with the cartoonishly big spoiler on the rear, across the top of the car to the front. Dmitri got the hood open, stared in wonder at the engine.

"I think this is the original engine!" he said.

"OK. I got it all on tape."

He pulled himself up directly to the embankment, using tree roots for handholds. He navigated around some leaking piles of insulation and metal drums.

"Can you believe it?" he asked. "A Superbird. I think it's the real thing, too, not a kit car. Sergei would know."

"Amazing," I said. "Let's go."

We started toward the fence, when there was a shift in a pile of junk. I didn't panic this time—it could be the wind, or an otter, or whatever. I turned just in time to see a three-foot-tall robot scuttling toward me.

I froze in disbelief and wonder. Even though it was

exactly what I was hoping to see, the sight of it stunned me. The robot was poised on two large feet and had folded forearms, flicking a long barbed tail. I could see why Sid compared it to a dinosaur. It glared at me with electric blue eyes.

Dmitri shoved me just as it fired, the eyes brightening as it let loose with a bolt of blue electricity. I felt a crackling in my shoulder; my muscles gave way, and I fell in a heap. I didn't lose consciousness—the Taser had just grazed me.

"Git!" said Dmitri, like he was scolding a stray dog. He grabbed a metal pole and hurled it. I quickly sat up and aimed the camera, which was still rolling. I'd forgotten to turn it off after scanning the car. I got a few seconds of the robot, but the camera was now flashing red for low battery.

The robot easily evaded the pole and now aimed its Taser eyes at Dmitri. I looked about for something to use as a weapon, but didn't see anything handy. I reached in my pocket and found the lump of blackened glass, heavy as a stone. I hurled it at the robot. The throw was short and wide, but the robot scurried away.

"Let's get out of here," said Dmitri, as if I needed the suggestion. We hauled it for the fence and crawled through. This time, I remembered my backpack.

"What do we do now?" asked Dmitri when we were past the railroad bridge.

"Pocket burgers?" I had just enough money left after buying the camera.

"I was hoping you'd say that."

CHAPTER 20

The restaurant had just opened and was empty. We sat at a table by the window, enjoying the greasy heat wafting over from the grill. I watched through the window, half expecting a battalion of dinobots to come flying across the street.

"Why did one come after me this time?" I wondered aloud. "They never bothered me before."

"Because you took something," said Dmitri. I remembered the lump of molten glass. It wasn't much to fight over. "It left us alone when you gave it back."

"Ha." *Gave it back* was a funny way to put it.

"They're like junkyard dogs," he said. "They protect their turf. They don't care if you're there, as long as you don't take anything. And the second you put something down, it's theirs."

"*Theirs*. So you think there's more than one?"

"Yep," said Dmitri.

"Me too."

"You guys are becoming regulars," said Sid. "One Roo, one Pig?"

"Sure," I said. The guy had a good memory for people and food.

"Fine with me," said Dmitri.

The camera battery was dead, so I switched to the AC adapter and plugged the camera into an outlet by the table—the same outlet that used to light up the hopping-kangaroo sign. I popped open the viewer.

"I want to see." Dmitri nudged the camera.

"After me." The viewer was too small for us both to watch at once. I rewound the video until I saw the car, then watched my herky-jerky camera work as we walked toward the fence, the blur of junk when I was tackled by Dmitri, and the final seconds of footage with the robot. I wished I'd zoomed in on the machine before it scurried away. It's hard to think about that kind of thing when you're completely freaked out and are under attack.

Would this convince a skeptical stranger of anything?

A few more customers came crashing in, hooting and shouting the way men do. "Hey, it's the Panther!" one of the men said, waving. It was Dan, the guy from the excavation company. He came to our table and clapped me on the back. "I hear your missing pal showed up, no worse for the wear?"

"A bit worse, but getting better," said Dmitri. He showed his hands, which were still scarred from the frostbite.

"Oh, wow. You're the guy." Dan offered a high five, but Dmitri left him hanging.

"My hand's still a little ouchy," he explained.

"No worries." He dropped his hand. "Dan Clouts."

"Dmitri."

"So glad you're all right." Dan noticed the camera, leaned in to get a better look.

"My brother Sergei is a regular here," said Dmitri. "Maybe you know him?"

"Huh?" Dan looked up. "Yeah. Good guy. Hey, enjoy your lunch. Go Panthers." He forgot about the camera and headed for the counter.

"Come on," said Dmitri. "My turn."

"Fine." I handed the camera over just as the food came. I bit into my stuffed burger and got a mouthful of flesh-searing molten cheese. I would never learn! I took a long drink of Coke, looked up just in time to glance through the plate glass and see a tow truck double-parking.

"Your brother is here."

Dmitri shrank, tried to disappear, but it was too late. Sergei barged in and came straight to our table.

"Why aren't you two in school?"

"We're working on a school project." I pointed feebly at the camera.

"What are you doing, making a documentary about hamburgers?" He grabbed the camera and stared at the screen. "What's this?" He looked at Dmitri. "Were you at that junkyard where you got hurt?"

Dmitri nodded slightly. "But it's fine. Nothing happened."

"What are you doing skipping school, Dim? You want to

be a dropout like me? End up at the alternative school for losers like Masha? Or maybe just get yourself killed by bums?"

"Masha's school isn't for losers," Dmitri muttered.

This was a family argument and none of my business. I focused on my burger, which had cooled enough to eat. I took careful bites, trying to taste it with the nonburned part of my tongue.

"You'd break Mom's and Dad's hearts," said Sergei. "Skipping school, trespassing, stealing. I don't get it."

Sid noticed him and came over to the table.

"I won't be able to stay," said Sergei. He handed him a couple of bills. "I'll pay for these truants, though. You guys go get in the truck. I'm taking you to school."

"Er. Thanks," I said. We'd fulfilled our mission, at least. We had the video. There was a dinobot on it. I doubted it would be enough to send SWAT teams and military forces into the old junkyard, but it might be enough to send a couple of police officers to investigate.

It turned out the school did call home, but I told Mom I'd been there and the school made a mistake. I had proof: I'd taken a math test in fifth period.

Penny walked into the office while I was importing the video. I wasn't dumb—I had the screen showing the video docked, and some homework open in another window.

"You did skip school," she whispered. "I saw you not get on the bus. What did you do?"

"I just met a friend," I told her. "We still went to school."

"Was it Rocky?"

"No."

"I bet it *was* her. Do you like her?"

"Not the way you mean."

"Well, you should. She's smart and makes robots and cares about animals."

"She's awesome," I agreed. "But FYI the friend I met is her boyfriend."

"Oh." She made a sad face and left.

I burned the video to a DVD. I wrote in all-caps on the DVD with a dark blue Sharpie, OLD NOMICON SITE, and popped the disc in a mailer. I wrote the address for the police department in the same style, put four stamps on it, and stowed it in my backpack. The next day I dropped it in the mail. Nobody could say I hadn't tried.

I saw Rocky at the bus stop on Wednesday.

"I don't want to talk to you," she hissed.

"Hey, I'm sorry about what happened," I told her. "I didn't even know we were cheating."

"I know about *that*," she said. "Your sister told me it was her idea. She sent me a message on Facebook."

"She did?" She wasn't even supposed to have a Facebook account. "Then how come you're mad at me?"

"Because you and my stupid boyfriend went off on a dangerous little adventure yesterday."

"Hey, we were careful."

"Sure you were. And you didn't even think to invite *me*."

"I just thought—I didn't want—"

"You didn't want a girl cramping your style."

"Being a girl doesn't have anything to do with it. I didn't ask Oliver either. I just didn't think you'd want to come."

"Well, thanks for not even asking," she said. She sat down next to someone else so I couldn't keep talking to her.

The truth was, I didn't ask Oliver because he wasn't talking to me. He'd ignored my Facebook messages and walked away from me when he saw me coming. I guess cheating at robots was an uncrossable line with him.

Dad tapped on my door after dinner.

"I'm headed to the neighborhood meeting," he said. "Why don't you come with me?"

"Sure." I dropped what I was doing—which was nothing—and followed him downstairs.

"Good luck!" Mom yelled as we left. I wasn't sure why we needed it.

The meeting was a block away, in an old garage that had been turned into a community theater. Lots of cars were parked in the lot, including a police car.

Dad had been going to the meetings for years, but I'd never been before. There were about thirty people inside, most of them old enough to be retired and have grandchildren. "These are good folks," Dad whispered. "Sometimes a few concerned people make all the difference."

There was a cop at the front of the room and a tiny woman with white hair. They both said "Hi" to my dad.

"Anna," Dad said. "Bob." He stopped to talk to them, so I went on up to the back. I wished I'd brought a book.

Dad was working the room, greeting everybody, handing out business cards. The people here seemed to like him. They told jokes I couldn't hear, but made Dad slap his knees. They got in earnest discussions about things that made him turn serious and nod in sympathy.

A few minutes later, Ted Whaley from the Laundromat walked in. He nodded hello to Dad and the others, then came up and planted himself right next to me. He still smelled of stale cigarettes and dirty laundry, but now he also reeked of alcohol.

"They're making a golem," said Ted. "You know what a golem is?"

"That guy in *Lord of the Rings*?"

"No, I mean the one made out of clay. 'Golem, golem, golem, I made you out of clay,'" he sang, then laughed. "It's a fairy tale."

"Um, OK." I'd never heard of it.

"They built a monster to defend themselves," he said.

"Oh."

Dad was sitting more up front, but he turned back to make sure I was there and paying attention. I wondered what I was supposed to get from this meeting.

Anna started the meeting by talking about meeting

minutes from last time, the final report of the holiday committee, and an open steering-committee position.

"Mr. Knox is the only candidate for the position, and will say a few words," she said. Dad was running for something?

He stood up and told a couple of jokes—about how cold it was, about how the garbagemen never put the cans back in the right spots. People laughed. Dad went on and said he'd lived in the neighborhood a long time, and thought it was a great place to raise a family, despite what anyone said. The people in the audience nodded appreciatively.

"I want you all to meet my son," he said. I had to stand up. People wheeled around to see me. I realized what this was all about. I was there to help humanize Dad. Just like when politicians posed with their whole family in TV commercials. He could have brought mom and Penny, too, but probably didn't want to overdo it.

"Well, since Mr. Knox is the only candidate for the position, we can just have a show of hands," said Anna. But before she could do it, the door swung open and Rocky's dad came in, stooping so he didn't bang his head on the low frame. "Sorry I'm late," he said. "Is it too late to throw my hat in the ring for this thing I read about in the newsletter?"

CHAPTER 21

Dad winced, then grinned and said he hoped there wasn't a real ring involved, because he could never take Mr. B. in a boxing match. There was a belated tittering. Mr. Blankenship had a chance to say a few words himself, and he only said a few—that he was a firefighter, lived right there (he pointed), and grew up over there (he pointed the other way). He wanted to join the committee because when he'd volunteered for cleanup after the tornado hit (clever how he slid that in), he'd gotten to know a lot of people and wanted to do more.

"Never vote for the good-looking guy," said Ted. He tapped his nose.

"I'll try to remember that."

"Well, maybe we can let people ruminate on both of our excellent committee candidates, and we'll vote at the end," Anna suggested. I let my mind wander as they talked about green spaces and early planning for the community garden and super-early planning for the summer cookout. They moved on to the police report. Bob the policeman recited the past month of local crimes: a couple of robberies, a rash of car thefts, a few domestic disturbances. Vandalism was down—people clapped, but I figured it was because of the cold. Who wanted to tag stop signs when it was below freezing?

"What about Sidney's?" shouted Ted, standing up. Heads cranked around to look at him. "They smashed up Sidney's!"

"There was some unexplained vandalism at Sidney's," Bob admitted. "We suspect it was random and incidental; there haven't been any other—"

"The hell there haven't!" Ted shouted. "Them dinosaurs did it is what happened. The ones you keep ignoring me about."

"Ted, please sit down and let Bob speak," Anna whispered.

"I want to know why they're ignoring the dinosaurs," said Ted.

The entire room bristled.

"Dinosaurs have been extinct for fifty million years," a man offered.

"Not these. They're machines," said Ted. "I've been watching them. One of 'em zapped me. Still got the scar." He planted a foot on the armrest and started to roll up his pants leg.

"That's not necessary," said Anna. "Ted, I'm sure if you wanted to wait until after the meeting, Bob would be happy to talk to you." Bob's face said otherwise.

"Look, Ted," he said, "we have your report, and we have

the DVD you sent. Be assured that we're doing the best we can to ascertain the problem and resolve it."

"You couldn't ascertain your own behind if you had an anatomy chart and a flashlight!" Ted said. I laughed. I was the only one who did, so I cut it short.

"Ted, if you don't settle down, we'll have to ask you to leave," said Anna. Rocky's dad and a couple of other men started to stand up, ready to bounce him out of there. Ted sat down and fumed.

"They aren't doing anything," he muttered. "Fools. And I never sent no DVD neither. Do they think I have a DVD recorder? Ha." He saw me looking at him. "You don't have to believe me, kid. You'll believe soon enough. When the dinos finish their golem, you'll believe."

"I already believe," I whispered. "I've seen one of the dinobots myself." But what was a golem?

Anna was calling for the vote—someone was ripping sheets of notepaper into strips for a silent ballot.

"How many of the dinobots are there?" I asked Ted.

"Five or eleven," he said.

"And what's the golem?"

"It's a big one. Reckon it'll lay waste to the neighborhood," he said.

I gulped.

The pieces of paper went around. I wasn't sure I was allowed to vote, but I took one anyway and wrote down Dad's name.

He lost the election, 34–3.

* * *

"Blankenship never even comes to meetings," Dad grumbled on the walk home.

"It's just a popularity contest," I said.

"I'm plenty popular," he said. I remembered him working the room, telling jokes and shaking hands. Now I saw the people's smiles as frozen, their laughter as forced. Had he ever gone on one of his rants in a meeting? Or maybe they saw him as a pushy salesman. It was hard to know.

"Do you know the dinosaur guy?" I asked my dad.

"Ted? Yeah, he's a real piece of work. He's at every meeting, talking about some made-up nonsense. What were you two talking about?"

"He asked me who to vote for, and I said you," I said. That wasn't true, but I'd seen Ted write Dad's name on the sheet.

"Great. Me, you, and the crazy guy. That's my voting bloc," said Dad. "You voted for me, right?"

"Of course."

"At least somebody voted for me who isn't crazy," he said.

I tried talking to Oliver the next day at school. I caught him at his locker.

"Hey, man."

He didn't even look at me. He traded a few books around and split.

Dmitri waved me over at lunch, encouraging me to sit

with him and Rocky, but Oliver was there. I didn't feel like eating Tater Tots in front of someone who hated my guts.

What was the big deal? Well, OK, sure. We'd cheated. Cheating was bad. Still, even if Oliver refused to believe I wasn't in on it, it wasn't like I'd drowned a bag of kittens. We didn't even get away with it. Oliver seemed to be taking the whole thing *way* too seriously. I would tell him so, but he wasn't talking to me.

I finished eating in about five minutes and went to the library. I had some social studies homework and figured I could get ahead on it. We were supposed to find some people in the news talking about the U.S. Constitution. Politicians were always saying stuff wasn't constitutional, so it would take about five seconds.

I went to the local newspaper website to get started, and a "breaking news" graphic caught my eye. There was a photo of First Street with two police cars, and yellow tape stretched across the shattered windows of the Laundromat.

Accidental Death Connected to Vandalism

Police are investigating the death of a laundry attendant in North Minneapolis. Theodore Whaley (62) was found dead at the Coin-Up Laundry at 4709 North First Street, the victim of an apparent cardiac arrest following a physical assault early this morning. It is believed that Whaley attempted to intervene when vandals attacked the establishment and had an electroshock weapon used against him. Such weapons usually have no permanent effect but can be deadly when used on people with heart conditions or neurological disorders. The police seek the assailants for charges of aggravated assault and second-degree murder.

This is the second reported case of vandalism on the 4700 block of First Street in recent weeks, the first occurring early in the morning last week at Sidney's Diner.

I printed the article and ran off to the cafeteria. Oliver was still sitting with Dmitri and Rocky.

"They got Ted," I told them, slamming the paper down on the table.

"Who's Ted and who got him?" Rocky asked.

"Ted is a guy and the dinobots got him," I said.

"Dinobots?"

"These robot dinosaur things. They're at that junkyard on Half Street. They must have been built by Nomicon once, and they're still there."

Dmitri grabbed the printout and read it. Oliver munched on his fish sandwich, pretending to ignore me, but I could tell he was listening closely. Rocky just stared at me.

"Dmitri's seen them, too," I said.

Dmitri set the pages down. "It's true," he said. "I saw one with Jim last week. And one of them zapped me when I tried to steal Jim's cameras."

"What? That was you?" Rocky gave him a hard look.

"Yeah." Dmitri looked helplessly at his scarred fingers. He'd forgotten she didn't know.

"Look, this is more important." I pointed at the printout from the newspaper website. "One of these things shot up Sidney's, and zapped Dmitri, and now they've *killed* a guy." There was a full minute of silence as the words hung heavily in the air. "We have to do something."

"Even if these things are real—" Rocky started.

"They are," Dmitri told her.

"Fine! The question is, what *exactly* are we going to do about them?"

Oliver finally spoke up. "That part is obvious."

"It is?" I asked.

"It is," he said. "We'll build our own robot."

PART IV

CUTIE

CHAPTER 22

Dad and I went to Ted Whaley's funeral service on Thursday morning. I wasn't sure Dad would let me go, since I had to miss half a day of school, but he thought it was a great idea.

"It's the neighborly thing to do," he said.

A dozen or so people were at the funeral home, scattered around the back half of the room. Anna from the neighborhood association was there, sitting with Bob the cop.

"Nobody else is here from the committee," Dad noted.

I did see Sid, sitting quietly with a sunlamp-tanned woman. I found out later she owned the Laundromat. She was one of the few to stand up and speak about Ted, when the funeral director invited people to do so.

The casket was open, and people drifted past to pay their last respects. Dad headed up, and I followed. It was the first time I'd seen a cadaver—Oliver's dad had had an urn, not a casket. Ted looked rosier and more cheerful than he had a few days ago. I was overwhelmed by it all: the weirdness of laying a dead body out for the world to see, the sadness of Ted's final moments in the world.

Dad let a hand rest on my shoulder.

"Death is a thing that happens," he said, grasping for something parental to say.

"I know."

Dad looked at Ted for a moment, shut his eyes and looked serious, then left me alone with the body.

I looked at his waxy, peaceful face. Based on his health and lifestyle, maybe he wouldn't have lived much longer. Maybe he wouldn't have accomplished much, either—a few more years of hard drinking, working a low-end job, showing up unwanted at neighborhood meetings, stealing donuts from the service station. Probably nobody expected Ted to turn his life around. What he'd lost was the chance to prove them wrong.

When I looked up, Dmitri and Sergei were there. They were both wearing black suits.

After the service, we moved to a separate room where there were cheese and crackers and olives on plastic trays.

"Should have had donuts and coffee," Sergei muttered as he looked at the fare. He fixed a plate, somehow ended up making small talk with Bob the policeman.

"I guess this is lunch," said Dmitri, making a cheese-and-cracker sandwich. "So, you knew Ted?"

"Barely," I admitted. "My dad knew him. Neighborhood group." I wasn't hungry, but nibbled on crackers for something to do.

"He put me up for a couple of days," said Dmitri. "After

what happened at the junkyard, he found me wandering around, frostbit and everything. Took me home and made me ramen and let me sleep on the couch. He only called the cops when he realized I had severe frostbite. He knew I needed a doctor."

"He said he just found you in the Laundromat."

"He was afraid he'd broken some kind of law," said Dmitri. "Harboring a fugitive or something. He didn't trust the police."

"Why didn't you just go home? Did you have amnesia or something?"

He looked around, saw that Sergei was safely out of earshot, but leaned in to whisper even more quietly. "At first. Then I was just ashamed to go home."

Dad pulled himself away from small talk, came and clapped me on the shoulder.

"Ready for school?"

We got to school at the tail end of lunch. Oliver was hanging around by my locker.

"Hey," I said.

"Hey," he said back, but he didn't move. "So, Penny really changed the program without you knowing?" I could hear doubt still simmering beneath the surface.

"Yeah," I said. "The kid is smart."

"All right," he said, his tone of voice saying otherwise. "I guess I believe you."

"Gee, thanks." I wondered if he was going to let me get at my locker. "I can't believe you'd think I'd do something like that. How long have we known each other?"

"I didn't think you'd dump me as a partner, either. Or steal from your dad and lie about it. Or let Peter bail you out. I didn't know how far you'd go."

"What's funny is you think cheating at robots is worse than all that other stuff." I finally got past him and opened my locker. "By the way, the funeral was lovely. Thanks for asking."

"Oh, right." His voice lost a little of its outrage. "Fine, I'm sorry I didn't believe you sooner. Even if you did all that other stuff, you never lied to me about any of it."

"Exactly." I traded a few books around and slammed the door closed. "Do you want to walk to class?"

"Sure." We headed down the hallway.

"I was just mad about losing," he admitted. "I don't know, maybe I'm not as smart as I think I am. That idea Penny had—I never would have thought of it."

"That's because you don't cheat."

"I wouldn't have thought of it, anyway," he said. "Next year I'm picking Penny for a partner."

"Hey, you could do a lot worse."

We went to Dmitri's after school to watch the video from Half Street. Dmitri had the camera wired up to play directly on the large-screen TV. Alexei stood right in front of the

TV, staring in fascination as Dmitri went back and forth over the same few seconds of footage.

"It looks like the velociraptors in *Jurassic Park*, only smaller," said Oliver.

"Real velociraptors *were* smaller than the ones in the movie," said Rocky. "I saw a fossil at the museum in Chicago. That thing is really similar to it."

"I'll bet Robbie could take it," said Oliver.

"It has a Taser," Dmitri reminded him. "It would toast your robot's circuits before it could throw one punch."

"Oh, yeah."

"Also, we don't know how many there are," I added.

"Good point again," said Oliver.

"We need to build a champion robot," said Dmitri. "One that can steamroll those things, even if there are a hundred of them. One that can take a few hits."

"Build it out of what?" Oliver asked. "A thousand Lego robot kits?"

"No," said Dmitri. "I thought we'd start with a car, then add stuff to it. Like I did with Viddy, but full-sized."

"I'll ask my Mom if we have any spare cars in the attic," said Oliver.

"No need." Dmitri was unfazed by Oliver's snarkiness. "We've got one in the backyard."

"Yeah, right," said Rocky. "Because Sergei doesn't even want that forty-year-old car that he spent every free minute of his life lovingly restoring."

"Don't worry about it," said Dmitri. "I have an idea."

Alexei must have understood what was going on, after all. He looked worried.

We met at the service station after it closed on Friday. I'd told Mom Oliver and I were going to see Sergei work on the Mustang, which was true.

"When did you get so interested in cars?" she asked.

"It's a '69 Mustang. It's awesome. And Sergei is really good."

"That does sound pretty cool," she said. "Don't be out too late."

When Rocky and Oliver and I got there, the Mustang was already up on the car lift.

"I can't believe he's letting us use the car," I said.

"Dmitri said he offered Sergei something in trade," said Rocky. "He was really mysterious about what it is."

Serge and Dmitri were talking about torsion rods and rear axles and the best way to disassemble a rolling chassis.

"They might as well be talking French," I admitted to Rocky.

"I *know* French," she said. "*Quel moyen de l'arrêt de bus? Je vais à la bibliothèque.*"

"Absolutely," I said. I had no idea what I was agreeing to.

I started wondering about the programming side of things. Could we use an ordinary-sized logic controller? What sensors would we use? What would we use for actuators? For that matter, what would the car use for weapons?

I realized Rocky was talking to me.

"I'm sorry," I said. "I didn't get any of that."

"I was saying that there's probably something more useful we could do than standing around."

"Sure," I said. "I know just the thing."

As I hoped, Dan Clouts was at Sidney's. His buddies were on the way out, but Dan seemed glad to have an excuse to hang around a bit longer.

"Sid! Round of sodas for my friends from Wellstone."

"Thanks, but that's not necessary—" Rocky tried to protest, but Sid was already plopping two pint glasses of cola on the table.

"Thanks, Captain Kangaroo!" said Dan.

"I told you not to call me that." Sid grinned anyway and headed back to the kitchen.

"I just call him that because of the—" Dan pointed at the window. "Aw man, I forgot it's gone."

"I miss it too," I told him.

"You know what happened, right?"

"Yeah. Vandals trashed the place. They also hit the Laundromat."

"The Laundromat—I almost forgot." He dabbed at his face with a napkin. "They killed Ted Whaley."

"You knew Ted?"

"He used to work for me." His voice fell quiet. "I missed the funeral. I should have gone."

"I went with my dad," I told him. "They were friends. Sort of."

"Poor, crazy Ted." He brooded in silence for a few seconds and forced a smile. "So what are you kids doing tonight?"

"Funny thing you should ask," I told him. "Because we're looking for . . . well, we're looking for a demolitions expert."

"No kidding?" His eyes narrowed. "What are you up to?"

I looked around to make sure nobody was eavesdropping and told him everything we knew. For some reason, I felt like he'd believe us.

"Nomicon," he said. "You know, that place has traded hands four or five times since the accident? At least one of the owners hired a crew to clean it up." He pointed at himself with his thumb. "We were the crew. And I can tell you, that place wasn't right. Equipment disappeared and broke down. Crazy stuff happened overnight. And then there's what happened to Ted." He stopped for a solemn moment.

"What happened?" Rocky whispered.

"He was a machine operator before he was a drunk. Well, he was a drinker already, but not on the job, or I wouldn't have had him around. Two days into the Nomicon job, he was the last one to leave at night. The next morning he didn't show up for work. Didn't show up the day after that, either. After six days I went to tell him he was fired. I found him in his apartment, half out of his mind—I think he'd been drinking, sure, but there was something else. He was scared of something. He wouldn't tell me what it was. But something happened to him at the site. I figured out that much. He said he didn't want to come back to work anyway. Well, we dropped the Nomicon project. Too much bad luck."

"So you believe us?" Rocky asked.

"And you can help?" I added.

"Tell you what," he said. "Come around Clouts and Sons tomorrow morning around ten."

"Thanks. We'll do that."

"I'm going to make a call," said Rocky. "Too noisy in here." She left. A moment later we could see her through the plate glass, talking on the phone.

"Got yourself a keeper there," said Dan.

"She's not mine to keep."

"Hey, be patient. Sometimes things work their way around."

"Maybe."

"Yeah, what do I know?" he said. "I'm past forty and single." He looked at his watch. "You know, let's make it nine tomorrow, all right? I have a lot of stuff to do."

"Yeah. Sure."

Rocky was waiting for me outside.

"Want to head back to the garage?" I asked.

"No, I better go home. My parents will be freaking out."

"Mine too," I said. "Did you tell Dmitri?"

"Yeah. He just wanted to make sure you were with me. He didn't want me to go alone."

We started walking. The worst of winter was behind us,

but there was a soft, water-globe-style snow falling, shining in the glow of the streetlights. I wasn't going to get a better chance than this.

"I like you a lot," I told her when we were almost home.

"I'm glad we've become friends," she said.

Dad had seen us through the kitchen window, looked at me when I came in and took off my boots.

"Was that the Blankenship girl?" He probably didn't like it, since he didn't like her dad.

"Um. Yeah. We hang out sometimes."

"I thought you were with Oliver."

"I was," I said. "We both were."

"You're kind of young to have a girlfriend," he said.

"Don't worry about it. That's not even close to happening."

CHAPTER 23

Dmitri messaged me early Saturday morning. Sergei was working at the shop all day Saturday and wouldn't be able to work on the robot until late that evening. "Not sure what to do until then," he wrote.

"Want to go look at demolition equipment?" I told him about meeting Dan.

"Sure. I'll ride in with my bro."

"I'll tell R." I said. I'd forgotten to tell her Dan moved the appointment back an hour.

"I got it," he said. "Chatting w/her in another window."

Mom stopped me on the way out.

"What's up? Where're you going?"

"We're going to watch Sergei work on the car some more."

Penny pretended to go on reading, but I caught her glancing up at us.

"You're really getting into this, huh?" Mom asked. "What is it with men and machines?"

"I don't know."

"Can I go?" Penny asked. "I like machines, too."

Mom shushed her. "Let Jim spend time with his friends."

"We'll do something when I get back," I promised.

"Be back by two," Mom said. "I have some errands to run."

"Will do."

By the time I got to the service station, Sergei already had a boxy car up on a lift and was working on the underside with a wrench.

"Those cars look like toasters," I said.

"Toasters have more horsepower." Dmitri was munching on a donut. "Have one. Serge says nobody eats them anymore."

Not since Ted stopped coming around, I thought. I took one with chocolate drizzled on top. It wasn't great, but it wasn't bad. Dmitri was also gulping a foam cup of foul-smelling coffee. I passed on that, but had a couple of paper cones of water to wash down the donut. The owner came in, wearing his grease-monkey coveralls, and started riffling through some papers behind the counter.

"Hey, what happened to the Mustang? Back at your place?" I whispered to Dmitri.

"Sergei rented a storage unit down the street," Dmitri explained. "He didn't want to keep towing it back and forth across the river."

"Good idea." The Nor-Stor-All was on First Street, a block or two north of Sidney's.

"Hey, how did you talk Sergei into giving it up?" I asked.

"I have my ways," he said.

The phone rang, and the owner grabbed it.

"Oh yeah? Well, when are you coming in? We have a tight day as it is. No, that's not acceptable." He got more and more worked up as he spoke. He reminded me of Dad.

"Let's go," said Dmitri.

"What about Rocky?"

"She's not coming. Said she wasn't even dressed yet and didn't want to hurry out just to look at junk."

"Oh, OK." That was surprising. She seemed to like junk.

We went outside. Clouts & Sons was on the other side of the lumberyard, and it only took us a few minutes to walk there. It was an ugly sprawl of gray concrete bunker-looking outbuildings and fences. The main building was closed, the windows dark. We rapped on the front door, and there was no reply.

We were a bit early. We paced to keep warm. Dmitri's phone beeped. He looked at it.

"Rocky?"

He nodded. "She says happy picking."

A dark green Dodge Ram turned into the parking lot. It was spattered with the gray-white road funk of salt-melted snow. It was Dan. He parked helter-skelter in the middle of the lot and rolled down the window.

"What we want is around back." He cruised on and we followed.

Behind the building were a couple of padlocked sheds. He opened one that seemed older and more neglected.

"Most of this stuff is useless to us," he said. "But it could be useful to you." He found the light wasn't working, swore at it, and heaved the door open more so sunlight could angle in. It didn't do much to illuminate the jumble of rusted metal.

Dmitri looked uneasy. "This is OK with the owner, right?

"Hey, it's my name on the sign. Don't worry about it."

"But are you *the* Clouts, or one of the sons?"

"I'm *the* Clouts," said Dan. "I inherited some money when I was thirty. All I ever wanted to do was wreck stuff, so I started this business. I let people assume I was the son, that there was some old guy running the show."

"Just making sure," said Dmitri.

"Yeah, well. Since you bring it up, you know, I didn't give you this stuff, OK? It's mine to give, but I don't want to get in trouble for giving it to kids. Hey, I think there's a bulldozer blade back here you can use." He eased around some equipment and disappeared.

Dmitri's phone beeped again. He checked it, made an *mm* noise, and texted something back.

"Rocky again?" I asked.

He nodded. "It's nothing."

"I found the blade!" Dan shouted from the back. "And I got a surprise for you. Let me get the forklift."

Oliver had told me to look for anything that could be

used as actuators, the muscles that let the robot's brain move its parts. I went to work on a backhoe, wrenching off the control panel and stripping the cables. They weren't much thicker than the gear and brake cables on a bike.

"Need a box for that?" Dan asked.

"Sure."

He removed a few bottles of motor oil from a case and passed it over.

His surprise was an enormous pear-shaped wrecking ball. It took Dan twenty minutes to unearth it from the rest of the old machinery.

I grabbed the ring on top and tried to move it. It didn't budge.

"It's heavy."

"Four hundred and seventy pounds," said Dan. "Small for a wrecker. We have a bigger one, but we couldn't get it on the truck. Not that my truck could haul a two-ton ball."

"The robot car couldn't handle that either," said Dmitri.

"Can you use it?" Dan asked. "It won't be a picnic getting this over there." I could see he was beginning to regret having showed it to us.

"We can use it," I told him. "It's perfect."

Dmitri had to get the key to the storage locker from Sergei. He said he'd meet us at the Nor-Stor-All. Dan and I drove over with the first load of stuff. As we waited, we saw a family hauling furniture from a rental truck into one of the sheds. A teenage girl pulled on her coat sleeves to bury her hands and leaned against the side of the truck while her parents carried battered boxes and garbage bags stuffed with clothes into the shed. A boy Penny's age tried to be super-helper, carrying a duffel bag as big as he was.

"Maybe they lost their house," Dan said in a low voice. "Tough times. Come on, let's help 'em out."

We got out of the truck. The wind blowing off the river had an icy bite to it and a slight fishy smell.

"We got nothing else to do while we wait," Dan told the family as he grabbed a box from the U-Haul. I grabbed one too.

"Very nice of you," said the mom.

The boy slowed down after a couple of loads. Maybe it sank in that his heroism wouldn't make a difference in the grand scheme of things.

"You're doing good work," I told him.

"It stinks!" he said.

"It sure does." I wasn't sure if he was talking about the fishy smell or the whole situation.

Dmitri helped when he got there, and the truck was empty in a few minutes. The dad pushed some bills on us, which Dan told us to keep.

"Let the guy have a little pride," he whispered to me.

Burger money, I thought. I could use it.

"Sergei says to be careful and not scratch the Mustang," said Dmitri as he unlocked the door.

"It's going to be wrecked anyway," I reminded him. In fact, the body of the car was already off the chassis. It was resting there, but not attached.

"He's still in denial," said Dmitri.

Dan and Dmitri worked the blade around the Mustang and stored it in the back. They'd also taken the arm from a small excavator. I learned from Dan that the back part of the arm was called the boom, and the front part was called a dipper. The shovel was missing, but we would use the arm to wield the quarter-ton wrecking ball.

"One more trip," said Dan.

A police car turned into the parking lot, slowly cruised up and down the lanes in front of the storage sheds. I saw through the window that it was Bob, Dad's friend from the neighborhood association.

"He's looking for break-ins," I guessed.

"Or families living in their storage units. It's been a Steinbeck novel around here lately." Dan waved hello at the police car and put the truck in gear.

CHAPTER 24

I stopped by Oliver's on the way home to give him the box of cables. He immediately took the back off the control panel and studied the circuits and switches. "This is perfect," he said. He hummed a cheerful tune as he started pulling out wires and chips. He had some other stuff already on the table: spools of black cable and a circuit board with a cracked case.

"What're those?"

"A kinematic controller from the hobby store and an adaptive panel that allows people with disabilities to drive."

"Which means . . ."

"Combined, they mean the robot brain can control the car."

"Cool." I watched him for a few minutes, envying his confidence as he went about his work.

"So, this must be the ultimate robot wars, huh?" I asked him. "Wouldn't you like to see this thing take on Rolf's egg?"

"Ha," he said. "That wouldn't be a fair fight. But yeah, this is a good challenge."

"A challenge," I echoed. "Oliver, do you think your father *made* those robots we're fighting?"

"He definitely did," he said. "Peter, too. They were both part of the team that built them. I emailed Peter, but he said everything he did at Nomicon is still top-secret."

"It must feel weird, building a robot to fight your dad's own robots."

"It is weird," he said. He focused on his work, but I could tell his chin was trembling. "You know, it's more like a mission than a challenge," he said.

"You don't think these robots caused the accident?"

"It doesn't matter. Nomicon did, and these things are what's left of Nomicon."

I glanced at the clock on the wall behind Oliver. "Oh, drat. I have to be home ten minutes ago. Anything I can do?"

"Start programming," he said. "You're good at it."

Oliver lent me his laptop so I could work on the program. He had special software to help write and debug the code. I went up to my room, the laptop under my arm, ready to get to work.

"You said you'd do something with me!" Penny wailed.

"Sorry, something came up."

"But I'm bored." She ran up the stairs after me. "Where did you get the computer?"

"It's Oliver's. He lent it to me."

"Why?"

"Because we're building a new robot and I'm programming it," I said without thinking.

"I want to help."

"No. Sorry. You can't this time." Penny was pretty sharp, but there was no way I could let her get mixed up with this. She was only nine.

"Can I at least *watch*?"

"You're going to watch me work on the computer?"

"Yes."

"Sounds boring to me, but be my guest." I opened Oliver's software and started clicking around, seeing how it worked. Penny's eyes were like two spotlights on me. I couldn't concentrate.

"Why don't you read a book or something?"

"OK." Penny looked at my books, took one at random. I didn't notice which one it was.

"This book is dumb," she decided after reading the back. She started to put it back, but a shiny circle rolled out. "What's that?"

"Nothing." I shoved the computer aside and tried to get to it first, but she was way too fast.

"It's a DVD. What's on it?"

"It's a horror movie. A guy at school lent it to me. It's really violent and disgusting."

"Cool! I want to see!" She took it and ran for the stairs.

Darn it, a few days ago the sci-fi book about the giant

fungus seemed like the safest place in the world to hide something. I put down the computer and went after her.

She already had the TV on and was putting the disc into the player.

"Penny, come on. It's private."

"Let me see what it is, or I'm telling Mom and Dad."

I sighed. "I thought you were done blackmailing people."

"Just let me see what it is, then. So I won't have to blackmail you." The junkyard flickered to life on the screen. "I know where that is," said Penny. "Did you go back? Are there otters?" She fast-forwarded, seeing the ruins of the building and the car. "This is boring."

"So stop watching."

She stopped when she saw the robot. "It's real," she said in a whisper. "I knew it! I thought I imagined it."

I could see the gears turning in Penny's brain.

"And you're building a new robot? What is it going to do?" She wasn't taunting me this time. Her voice was steady and serious. She sounded like Mom in the middle of an interrogation.

"Nothing. Just robot games."

"Tell me what it's going to do, or I'm telling Mom—"

"It's going to paddle little sisters who don't mind their own business." I ejected the DVD and headed upstairs. Penny didn't follow me, and didn't fight anymore about it, so I should have known she was up to something.

* * *

I was bleary-eyed and half asleep on Monday at the bus stop. I'd been up late figuring out robot mechanics and remembered too late that I hadn't done a scrap of homework.

"Hey," said Rocky. "How's *your robot*?"

"OK," I said. Why did she sound angry?

"You blew me off on Saturday," she said. "I waited and waited for you to call, then I realized you'd left without me."

"What?" Dmitri had told me she didn't want to come. He must have lied to me, to keep her from coming. "I'm sorry, we should have invited you."

"I want to be a part of this!" she said. "I really like robots, OK? I like making things. I like programming. Plus, I've been using power tools since I was ten. I have skills, man. I can do stuff."

"I know. Seriously."

"Dmitri says there's no room at the garage," she said. "Do you want help with the program?"

I thought about it. I'd been able to work with Penny on the last robot because she was always there, from the beginning, and learned the program along with me. Even then it was like trying to tie a shoe with someone else, each of you taking one lace. My new code was an undocumented mess, full of variables and functions I'd made up on the fly. I wouldn't know how to divide the job up and share it.

I took too long to answer. Rocky started punching me in the arm. "You too! You boys are all alike."

"No we're not. Stop it." I held a hand out, caught her

fist. I held on to it a moment longer than I needed to. She let me a moment longer than she needed to, then pulled her hand back.

"I'll find something to do," she said, "whether you like it or not."

Dmitri brought Viddy to school on Wednesday. Viddy was similar to the robot we were building, and I could use it to check my code.

"Have you seen Rocky?" he asked me.

"Not since Monday."

"Hmm. She must be sick."

"Must be? You haven't talked to her either?"

He lowered his voice. "She dumped me."

"Oh." I forced myself to frown. "That's too bad."

"It's OK. We're still friends." I had a feeling it wasn't OK.

He patted the box with Viddy. "Don't let this little guy get hurt. I've grown attached."

"Of course," I told him. "I'll treat it like my own robot."

As soon as I got home, I uploaded the program to Viddy's logic controller. I'd already mapped the inputs to its sensors and outputs to its actuators.

First I tested Viddy on the table, making sure he wouldn't roll off the edge.

"Awesome!" said Penny, as the car flew back and forth across the table, braking and turning when it reached an edge.

"Proof of concept," I told her, using one of Oliver's expressions. I would use the same setup to make sure our giant robot wouldn't sail off the ledge and crash down on the riverbank. "It's when you do something just to prove you can do it. Now let's see if it can bat stuff up."

"Cool," she said. "I want to help."

I fashioned a dipper and boom from parts in Oliver's box of robot gear and rigged it up on Viddy's rear end. I tested it on windup toys in the upstairs hallway—it took a few trials and errors, and frantic moments of debugging the code, but soon Viddy could chase down the windup toys and knock them over. The sensors worked together to find things that moved, calibrate their height, even get a basic sense of their shape. I set off a windup frog. It took three hops before the robot zoomed in and knocked it sideways, helplessly kicking its legs.

"Jim, what concept are you trying to prove?" Penny asked.

"Never mind." I wound up a monkey and set it loose. The robot watched it clack by without making a move.

"It likes monkeys?" asked Penny.

"It looks more like a person," I explained. "We want the robot to ignore things shaped like people. That's what I'm testing."

"Hm. What about the otters?"

"Good point. I'll have to protect them, too."

"Aha!" She stabbed an index finger into the air. That's

when I knew she'd guessed what we were up to, and how I accidentally told her she was right.

Penny and I went to the Nor-Stor-All on Saturday to see the robot. Dmitri had told Sergei we were coming.

"I'm not crazy about this idea," Sergei told us. "We're not doing nickel shows."

"I'm not giving you a nickel," said Penny. "My price is keeping it a secret."

"We have five minutes before I go to work," said Sergei. He opened the storage-locker door.

In front of us was the biggest and most dangerous robot I'd ever seen. The dipper and boom were now mounted on back, the blade installed in front. The car was jacked up on truck-sized tires so the blade fit beneath the grille. The robot looked like a giant crocodile with a crooked tail and a bad overbite.

"Wow." Penny gave it an awed look.

"It's amazing," I said. "What about the ball?"

Sergei explained that he'd need to add some reinforcement to the frame, and use a hydraulic lift to get it up there. He was saving that part for last, since it would be dangerous to work on the car with a quarter-ton ball hanging over it.

Penny crouched in front of the car, patted the hood as if it was the head of a big, friendly dog.

"What a cutie," she said.

The name stuck.

* * *

I worked late into the night on Oliver's laptop. I was able to wijack Internet access from the coffee shop across the street, and kept my IM open. At about two a.m. a message popped up.

Rochelle: u up?

Jim: yep.

Rochelle: need to talk. meet me outside?

Jim: rly?

Rochelle: lots to say. don't want to type it all.

Jim: 2 m.

I changed from my hanging-around-the-house sweats into outside clothes, walked carefully down the stairs so I didn't wake anyone. Rocky was waiting for me, hugging herself and shivering.

"My parents would freak if you came in," I told her.

"I know. Same here. Let's just walk."

"Sure."

She walked toward Osseo Road. I followed. The intersection that was usually crowded with impatient cars was now deserted, the lights flashing red. We crossed, ignoring the sign with the red slash through a guy walking.

"Dmitri says you two broke up?" I ventured.

"He's a nice guy, but he thinks girls should stay at home and make cookies."

"Maybe it's a Russian thing?" I suggested.

"I don't care what it is," she said. "I don't want to make cookies, and nobody gets to tell me what to do just because I kissed him a couple of times."

Only a couple of times?

"Besides," she said, "he lied to me and kept a bunch of secrets and makes excuses for all of it."

"Is that what you want to talk about?" I asked. Had I become her confidant?

"No, this is more important," she said. "I found something to do, just like I promised."

"What?"

"Research. Some of it at the U's engineering library, and some actual field research. Do you know what kind of business Nomicon did?"

"They made robots and other stuff."

"They made *war* robots and other *war* stuff," she said. "I found a story about them in a journal on military engineering. These robots were for recon missions. The idea was to drop them into a combat zone and let them gather up the useful supplies. The robots would protect the cache until somebody came to collect."

"And it looks like they're pretty good at it," I said. "Is the Army using them now?"

"Nomicon made four prototypes, then the project was cut."

"Why was it cut? Those robots are brilliant."

"The accident shut down the company," she said. We passed in front of the elementary school and onto the playground. Oliver and I played here as kids, but all of the equipment was new. Rocky grabbed the cold chain of a swing and sat down. I took the swing next to her, stretching my feet out.

"The robots had rules," she said. "They're supposed to protect the perimeter of their territory and lay low. They let people come and go, but don't let them take anything. They're programmed to stun, not to kill."

"What about Ted Whaley?" They'd not only killed him, they'd left their territory to do it.

"That's what they were *programmed* to do," she said. "But I think after being feral for so long, they've . . . evolved. They've reprogrammed themselves."

"They adapted," I said. Just like the robots Rolf had talked about.

"That's what evolution is," she said. "Adaptation."

A chorus of police sirens sounded, speeding down Osseo Road. We watched them pass, not trying to talk over the noise. The sirens faded as they went south.

"I didn't tell you about my field research," she said. "I spent the day there, today, hiding and watching."

"Like Jane Goodall?"

"I don't know if Jane Goodall was ever shot at by chimps, but otherwise, yeah."

"You were shot at?" An icy wave passed through me.

"Don't worry. They missed."

"You shouldn't have gone there alone," I told her. "It isn't safe."

"It wasn't safe for you or Dmitri, either. Anyway, you don't know the worst of it."

"Why? What did they do?"

"Not what *did* they do," she said. "What are they *doing*. I know it doesn't make sense, but I swear they're building a robot of their own. A big one."

CHAPTER 25

Oliver looked more than ever the mad scientist. His hair was a lopsided bird's nest, his shirt was buttoned wrong, and his glasses were smudged and dusty.

I wasn't one to talk. I'd barely slept myself.

"I was up late finishing and testing the actuators," he said. "Are you done with the code?"

"Mostly," I said.

"We've got news," said Rocky. "And it might change everything."

We went up to Oliver's room. Rocky took some pens and scratch paper from the desk, moving Danny the stuffed bear out of the way so she could sketch.

"Nighttime can be scary, but it doesn't last forever," Danny said in his deep, calm voice. "Be brave, Junior. Try to sleep and dream good dreams." He started to hum a lullaby. I'd never heard that loop before, and I'd heard everything else the bear did a thousand times.

"What's that all about?" asked Rocky.

"Nothing," said Oliver. "Power off, Danny." The bear fell silent.

"Nice toy," she said.

"It is," said Oliver. "So what's your news that changes everything?"

"There's a robot we didn't know about," said Rocky. She drew as she talked. "It's a big box with arms and legs. Lots of arms, with fists." She drew a square, radiating long arms, and cube-like fists at the end of each arm.

"When I saw them, they were just dangling there, but if they work . . ." She shuddered.

"Where did you see it?" Oliver asked.

"In the first building. The one that's wrecked."

"You went inside?"

"Yeah. I had to." She finished drawing the robot and passed him the paper. "It didn't have a head, at least not yet. And it was already three stories high."

"If it's that tall, how did they put it together in an old office building?"

"They ripped holes in the floors," said Rocky. "The floors are like scaffolding now."

"Did you see any of the robots actually working on it?"

"Yes. That's the only reason I was able to sneak in. They were distracted. Do robots do that? Make other robots?"

"Sure," said Oliver. "Robots can do anything you program them to do."

"What are we going to do?" I asked. "We programmed our robot to fight little robots, not a great big Goliath robot." Or a golem robot, as Ted had called it.

I had a second thought I kept to myself: The robots had come after Ted. He hadn't taken anything, but he had seen their golem. Now Rocky had seen it, too. My hands were shaking. I shoved them in my pockets.

"Cutie won't be able to beat a giant," I said. "We need explosives or something."

"A better strategy is to finish Cutie before they finish making this thing," said Oliver.

Rocky's phone beeped. She dug it out of her pocket and frowned at the message. "Sergei's been arrested."

We piled into Oliver's mom's car to go see Dmitri. She wasn't excited about running a taxi service first thing on a Sunday, but we talked her into it.

Dmitri had the door open before we got up the front walk.

"The police came early this morning and woke everyone up," he told us. "It was scary. Alex had a seizure, right in the living room, while the cops were stomping around."

Rocky laid a supportive hand on his arm. He looked like he hadn't slept. He was a good match for the rest of us.

The house was askew. It was obvious the furniture had been moved around, the drawers rummaged through. Dmitri told us the police had charged Sergei with multiple counts of grand theft auto, but didn't tell any of us what evidence they had. They just cuffed him, read him his rights, and dragged him away.

"I guess I'll ask about the elephant in the middle of the room," said Oliver. "Dmitri, is Sergei guilty?"

Dmitri took a deep breath and exhaled slowly. "I don't think so," he said.

"You don't *think so*?" Rocky asked. "You don't know if your own brother is a car thief?"

"It's complicated," said Dmitri. "There's stuff about him I never told you."

Mom and Dad were waiting for me when I got home.

"What's going on?" I hung up my coat. "I was just at Oliver's. I left a note."

"For starters," said Dad, "you ask for *permission* when you leave. You don't just scribble something on the board and take off."

"Sorry. I didn't want to wake you up."

"For another," he said, "we called Oliver's house and you weren't there. His mother said she'd just dropped you off at this—what's his name?"

"Dmitri."

"Whom we already know is mixed up in something," said Dad. "He goes missing, and the guy who finds him is dead. And now his brother is in jail."

"What? You know about that?" Had it been on the news?

"I talked to Bob," said Dad. "He called me because he knows you've been hanging out with those boys."

"Just with Dmitri," I said.

"Is Sergei the tow-truck driver who gave you and Penny

a ride home one night?" Mom asked. "The same boy you keep going to see, working on that muscle car?"

"Yeah, but he just saw us that one time and gave us a ride. And he is rebuilding a car, but we just watched. And he's probably innocent." I remembered the Audi in his backyard, which might have been Peter's car after all. "Even if he's guilty, it's got nothing to do with Dmitri."

"I don't want you spending time with hoodlums," said Dad. "I don't want you taking rides from them, or going to their houses, or . . ."

"Or inviting them to our house," Mom added. "This Dmitri seems to be mixed up with a lot of questionable things."

"Fine," I said. "I have so many friends, I might as well tell one to go stuff himself." I started up to my room.

"You don't talk like that to us!" Dad yelled.

"I do when you're wrong," I shouted back. I went in my room and slammed the door. I would have understood if Dad stomped up the stairs after me and shouted for an hour, but this time he didn't.

"Do you have the key to the storage shed?" Oliver asked Dmitri at lunch the next day.

"No," said Dmitri.

Oliver leaned in. "Did Sergei have it on him when he got arrested?"

"I don't know. It's not the main thing on my mind."

"Maybe it should be," said Oliver. "If the police have the

key, they're going to go check out the unit. They'll find Cutie."

"The police searched his room," said Dmitri. "They must have the key."

"We can't wait, then," said Oliver. "We have to get the robot before they find it."

"What are we supposed to do," asked Rocky, "break into the unit?"

"I don't know, but this is a really bad development." Oliver stabbed up some peas with his fork.

"Well, I'm bored with robot games anyway," said Dmitri. He shoved his untouched tray of food out of the way and left the table.

"It's not a game," Oliver said, too late for Dmitri to hear him.

I found Dmitri in the library, checking his email on the computer.

"Hey." He acknowledged me, but went on reading his email. I pulled up a chair.

"Updates?" I asked.

"Mom says they can't make bail," he whispered. "Not unless Dad sells the Caddy."

"I'm sorry to hear that."

"If Sergei was stealing cars for real, we'd be loaded," said Dmitri. "They fix it so only the criminals can get out. Makes a lot of sense, huh?"

"Yeah. I mean, no."

"Do you think he's innocent?"

"Sure." I *wasn't* sure, but I didn't see the point in arguing. "Look, I'm sorry about your brother. But we can't give up on what we're doing. It's important."

"I'm not going to make any more trouble for my family," he said. "Sergei is gone. Alex has regressed about two years. Masha is having trouble at school. I can't add to everyone's stress."

"But there's stuff you don't know," I whispered. I told him about the golem. "Ted saw it, and they came after him. Now Rocky's seen it, too. What if they come for her?"

"That's not going to happen."

"We don't know that," I told him. "Look, I don't want you to make more trouble for your family. Just help us get the key back."

He closed his eyes, rubbed his forehead. "I do care about Rochelle," he said.

"I know."

He opened his eyes, lowered his hand. "They have a key machine at the service station, for people who want to copy car keys. The storage-locker keys say 'Do not copy under penalty of law,' but Sergei makes his own rules sometimes."

He reached in his pocket, came up with an oval green-and-gold Packers fob dangling a single copper-colored key.

"You guys do what you need to do."

* * *

Oliver and Rocky installed the actuators. Rocky worked the tools while Oliver explained how to rig up all the cables and controllers. I rolled up and down the lot of the Nor-Stor-All on my barely-used skateboard while they worked. If a car turned into the lot, I would roll over and tap on the door so they'd quit making noise. So far, there hadn't been any cars.

Most of the snow had disappeared from Minneapolis over the past few weeks, but people who grew up here know better than to get their hopes up and assume winter is done. Sure enough, a brisk snow started falling. I kept up my skating charade, even though it meant getting a faceful of icy crystals.

A police car turned into the lot. I rolled by the storage unit door, tapping on it as I passed. The cop car tootled along slowly and stopped next to me. The officer rolled down the window.

"Aren't you Willie Knox's kid?" It was Bob the policeman.

"Um. Yeah."

"What's up?" he asked, friendly and light, but I suspected he wasn't asking as a friend of my dad's. He was asking as a cop who knew I'd been hanging out with suspected felons.

"Skating," I said. "This is a good place to practice."

"There's a sign back at the entrance. No skating or biking."

"Oh. I didn't notice. Sorry."

"I hate to bust your chops about it," he said. "Tell your dad I said hi." He rolled up the window and turned the car around, parked in the lot and went into the manager's office. I rapped a bunch of times on the door so Oliver and Rocky knew the coast still wasn't clear, then skated past the police car. I figured it wouldn't be a good idea to still be there when he got back. I hid behind the farthest row of storage units and waited. I raked snow out of my wet hair with my ungloved hand. I'd left the hood to my parka at home, plus my scarf.

Officer Bob came back out a few minutes later, sat in his car, and radioed someone, then sat around some more.

I texted Rocky.

Stupid cop outside won't leave.

She texted back.

OK. Let us know when it's safe.

The snow slowed the evening traffic on First Street to a halt. A train was going by, backing up the cars for two or three blocks. Bob sat in his car, and sat in his car, and sat in his car.

Why? I wondered, and *Why now?*

Two more police cars were just across the tracks, waiting for the train. I caught glimpses of their flashing lights in between the boxcars.

A driver waiting on our side got tired of waiting, veered

into the left lane to do a U-turn, and floored it. The car skidded on the fresh snow and sailed past a stop sign. Bob flipped on his siren and was gone.

I sent a text.

Now!

The traffic gate went up as the train chugged on into the snowy night.

Oliver and Rocky hurried out of the storage unit, slammed the door, and ran across the lot to join me. The two cop cars turned into the lot and idled, wipers on.

"Do you think they have Sergei's key?" Rocky asked. "Is that why they're here?"

"That's what I'm afraid of."

Bob drove back into the lot, talked to the two other cops through the window, handed them something, and drove away. The police parked their own cars and climbed out. They went to one of the units and tried a key in the lock. After wiggling and jiggling, they moved on to the next unit.

"Oh crap crap crap crap crap," said Rocky.

"I know," said Oliver.

They were on the wrong row of units, but presumably would try every door before they gave up. If we were going to cook up a plan, it would have to be quick.

The key turned in a lock. One of the officers pumped his fist as the other slid the door open. They stared in disappointment and confusion at battered furniture and over-stuffed boxes of junk. It was the unit belonging to that family I'd helped. One of the cops took a toy out—a stuffed elephant in overalls—and gave it a curious look. Whatever the cop wanted to know, the elephant wasn't talking. He dropped it back into the box, stepped out, and closed the door. They went to the management office for a few seconds, then got in their cars and drove away.

"What happened?" Rocky asked. "That wasn't Sergei's key?"

"Or one key opens multiple units," said Oliver.

"In that case, they'll be back," said Rocky.

"I'm sure they will be," I agreed. "We have to move the robot."

"I have a better idea," said Oliver. "Let's finish this tonight."

CHAPTER 26

We stopped in at Sidney's. It was a slow evening—just Sid and a few regulars, including Dan Clouts.

"Get at least an inch an hour until tomorrow noon," Dan was telling Sid in his booming voice. "It'll melt down into slush, then freeze up. Roads will be a hockey rink by tomorrow morning, then you get snow on top of that." He shook his head. "I love Minnesota!"

I felt my back twinge at the mere thought of dealing with that much wet, heavy sludge when I got home.

"This sucks," I muttered.

"No, it's *perfect*," Oliver whispered. "The Nor-Stor-All will be deserted."

"Plus school will be canceled," Rocky added. "We can work all night if we have to."

"Good points, but there's another problem," I told them. "I haven't finished programming the robot."

"So finish it," said Oliver. "You have the laptop. We'll go work on the actuators while you do that."

"Sounds like a plan," said Rocky.

"Sure." I wasn't at all confident I could finish the code in time, but I would try. I took out the laptop.

We ate quickly—Rocky settling for the meatless veggie-stuffed burger once again, Oliver and I munching on Sid classics. He read over my shoulder and gave advice while I typed, which kind of slowed me down.

"Oh! I've got to call my parents," said Rocky. She got on her cell phone and called home, left a message saying she was at a friend's house. She called her friend to let her know she was a cover story.

Oliver called his own mom and said he was snowed in at Dmitri's house. He then texted Dmitri to let him know.

"Your house is too close," he explained. "Mom would just tell me to bundle up and walk home. You should say you're across the river for the same reason."

"I can't," I said. "They don't want me hanging around with anybody named Volkov."

"That's dumb," said Rocky.

"I know."

"Do you have any friends across town?" she asked.

"No, you are pretty much all of my friends in the world, right now. You two."

"Oh." Rocky played with her phone. Oliver munched on his burger.

Dan was getting bundled up to head into the cold. He nodded hello at us, but looked like he was in a hurry to get out.

"I'll face the music later. We have to focus on the robot. How much more time do you need with the actuators?"

"About an hour, maybe closer to two," said Oliver. "Then all we have to do is . . ." He smacked his forehead with his palm and groaned.

"What?" asked Rocky.

"We have to hang the wrecking ball," he said.

Dan had the door open, paused to stare in wonder at the fast-falling snow, and went outside.

"Hey, wait!" I shouted. I ran out into the snow and caught up with him.

Dan wasn't excited about extra driving in the snow, but he said he had just the thing. He left with Rocky and Oliver while I stayed at the diner and slogged through the code on the laptop. The different parts of the program both worked—one to find and wallop dinobot-sized machines, the other to explore the territory without nose-diving into the river—but I was still trying to make the two parts work together. More importantly, if a giant robot appeared, I wanted Cutie to stay the heck away from it.

The snow kept falling, and Sidney's emptied.

"I'd like to close up and get out of here," said Sid.

"I know, I know. Is the Laundromat open?" I could work there.

"They started closing at six after what happened to Ted."

I groaned. I couldn't work in the full brunt of the snow. Could I squat in the corner of the storage unit?

"Look, kid. It's OK if you hang around. The door will lock behind you. You guys stay safe, all right?"

"We will."

"You know, Dan has told me more than he probably should've," he said. "I know you kids are building some kind of contraption out of spare parts."

"A robot," I said. "A big one."

"I used to build stuff when I was a kid. We had this tiny house but a great big yard, and I had to mow it. I wanted a rider mower, but my dad said they cost too much and weren't worth it. So I tried to make one out of a bike, a toboggan, and a manual mower."

"Uh-oh." It wasn't hard to see where the story was going.

Sid pulled up his shirt to show me part of a long, ugly scar coursing across his side. "Some things are obvious in a hospital room that aren't obvious in the design phase," he said. "I guess I'm saying, try to think ahead to what might land you there yourself. But whatever you're doing, as long as nobody and nothing gets hurt, I say go for it. We didn't get to the moon because people were chicken." He grabbed his coat and headed for the back door. "It's OK to leave the lights on," he said. "Everything else is turned off and put away."

"Thanks!" I shouted as he banged out the back door.

I worked for another hour, then trudged back to the Nor-Stor-All in ankle-deep snow. I had never seen the city more deserted. The storage-unit door was wide open, the full-sized crocodile robot pushed out into the snow.

Dan was long gone, with whatever machine he'd used,

but the tail now had a stinger. The full size and weight of the thing was more evident when it was hanging overhead.

"Gimme," said Oliver, reaching out for the laptop.

I gave it to him. He'd already nested the logic controller deep in the car, packed into a pet carrier crammed full of bubble wrap and buckled into the backseat. A USB cord was threaded through the layers of padding and poked out the side. Oliver plugged the laptop into it and uploaded the code. When he was done, he stowed the laptop in the shed and pulled the door closed.

"Now what?" asked Rocky.

"We go to war," said Oliver.

"I mean, how do we get to Nomicon?" said Rocky.

"Oh yeah." I'd programmed that thing for robot battles. Not for driving around. It was hardly going to roll neatly out of the parking lot, keep right, and use a turn signal.

"Crap. I guess we have to drive it." Oliver peered into the car. "Do either of you know how to drive a stick?"

We looked at each other. Rocky tentatively raised her hand. "Kind of?"

"Let's roll," said Oliver.

We piled into the car. The Mustang moved in lurches at first, as Rocky figured out the pedals and clutch. She cruised out onto First Street, drove a block, and turned on her signal at West Bank Road.

"What are you waiting for?" Oliver asked. "There's nobody coming."

"But I'm turning left."

"You don't have to stop to turn left if there's no one coming."

"Hey, I don't know the rules," she said. "It's not like I have a license." She turned the wheel, punched the gas, and we skidded through a clumsy turn. She barreled down the middle of West Bank Road, Cutie's blade plowing the snow out of our path.

"This is pretty awesome," I said.

She turned again. The car came to a jarring halt as the blade hit the pylons—the motor groaned as the back tires spun in the snow.

"Uh-oh. There's no traction," said Rocky. "I have to reverse." We jolted backward. Rocky lurched back and forth until Cutie's blade had plowed out a path, then rolled at the pylons again. This time the back tires dug in while the blade plowed under the pylons and rolled them out of the way.

"Powerful car," said Oliver. "Lots of, uh, horsepower or whatever."

"Yeah, it must have a lot of cylinders," I said.

"Nice car talk, guys." Rocky turned on the headlights as we plunged down Half Street.

She braked when we reached the fence, and maneuvered the car to clear the snow in front of the gate. She stopped, the car's nose pointing at the gate, but left the motor running.

"This is where we all get out," she said. "Is the robot turned on?"

"It will be." Oliver threw a switch, and we all leaped out, slamming the doors behind us.

Cutie idled, her headlights cutting through the fence and lighting up the junk beyond.

"Well?" shouted Oliver.

"It's on a timer," I shouted back. I set the program to pause sixty seconds, so whoever threw the switch could get safely out of the car. I started counting down. When I got to thirty, my phone rang.

I fished the phone out of my pocket and saw the number. I hit the button and shouted over the roar of Cutie's giant engine.

"Hey, I'm OK. Sorry I didn't call sooner."

"Jimmy, thank God you're OK." It was Mom. "What's that sound?"

"It's just a car motor," I told her.

Whatever she said was lost in noise as Cutie charged the fence.

CHAPTER 27

The gate smacked down into the snow. Cutie rolled over it and into the piles of junk, sending a wake of snow and debris off to the side. She paused and waited for the enemy to approach.

"Jim!" Mom shouted. "What was that? Are you OK?"

"Yeah, yeah. I'm fine," I told her. "Look, I'm OK, but I might not be home until late. I love you guys." I turned off the phone and shoved it back in my pocket.

Something creaked and groaned down by the river. Cutie's engine revved up as her sound sensors put her on alert. A huge crash made the ground shudder, followed by another, and another, regular but unsteady. The golem was coming to greet us.

The three of us waited by the fence and watched. What I saw first was the head—a massive ball of smoky glass, like the lump I'd found in the building. From deep within it sparkled blue fire that lit up the night.

"What is that, a Tesla ball?" asked Rocky.

"I think it's a giant battery," said Oliver, his voice full of awe.

Then we saw the robot's arms—tentacles of hammered metal, lashing like whips. Each ended in a cube-shaped fist of white or silver: old washers, dryers, and squat refrigerators. There were eight of them, two per side of the body, which was made of corrugated steel from the shell of an old train car.

"It's an octopus," I said.

"Actually, it's a dodecahedrapod," said Oliver. "Twelve arms and legs."

"Whatever."

The golem reached the top of the embankment. Cutie charged.

"No!" cried Rocky. Cutie didn't stand a chance against this monster.

I realized there was also a dinobot there. Cutie knocked it sideways and sped on. She spun around just as she reached the bank. Her tail caught the golem in the kneecap and made it wobble. I felt a momentary hope that the golem would tumble backward, down the embankment, but it stomped on and rained blows on Cutie's head. It got three or four licks in before she sped away.

The golem also flattened the dinobot in the process, but compared with this thing, the dinobots were a mere nuisance. In the halo of blue light from the golem, I noticed another dinobot perched on a large drum, intently watching the fight. I stepped over to the fallen gate.

Rocky reached to grab me, but missed.

"*What are you doing?*" she shouted.

"I want to see something!" I crossed the gate into the junkyard, reached down, and made a snowball. I hurled it at the drum and hit it dead center. The dinobot leaped up and came after me. Cutie screeched by, scooped the dinobot up with her shovel, and drove it into a snowy pile of lumber. She turned, dropped the quarter-ton weight, and flattened the dinobot.

The golem stopped cold, midstep. Just as I hoped.

"They're cheating!" I shouted.

"What?"

"The dinobots are cheating. Their robot is remote-controlled! If we can knock out all of the little ones, we'll stop the big one." The golem was still frozen, but I had a feeling it wouldn't be for much longer.

"Knock them out how?" Rocky asked. "They fire lasers, remember?"

"Keep them moving so Cutie can see them. She's programmed to take them out."

Cutie's engine quieted to a purr as she rolled back into the middle and waited for more prey. Oliver and Rocky walked over the gate to join me. I reached down and packed another snowball.

The golem twitched. One of the other dinobots had taken the reins.

"Oh, and another thing," I said, pointing at the golem. "Watch out for that thing."

It roared back to life and sent Cutie on retreat. She

pushed through some junk toward the left side of the embankment. The golem stomped after her. Cutie reached the ledge, turned and roared back toward the golem. She suffered a few hits before turning again and heading back to the ledge. She was cornered! There was a gap between the robot and the bank where she could escape, but she couldn't find it. I cursed my lousy program.

I heard a crunching noise. I turned and saw Rocky swing a pole at another dinobot. It scuttled away from an upended pile of wood, wheeled around, and took aim—but it had landed right in the crease. Cutie saw it and charged, scooting right by the golem. She buried the robot under a pile of junk and turned around. The dinobot scuttled out of the debris, just to get crushed by Cutie's wrecking ball.

I held up three fingers, then one. Three down, one to go.

The last dinobot zipped out of hiding. Cutie gave chase, the dinobot hurrying toward the right side of the embankment. It leaped and landed on a fallen tree.

It's trying to lure her off the ledge, I realized. She braked, but too late. Her rear tires went off the ledge as she spun around in the snow.

The golem stomped over and laid into Cutie, punching her and pushing her farther off the ledge. Her rear wheels spun helplessly.

"Next time we use a four-wheel drive," said Rocky.

"Yeah. Next time," said Oliver. He picked up a snowball and hurled it at the dinobot, missing by a mile.

The golem took a swing at Cutie's tail with one of its long arms and knocked the wrecking ball loose from the dipper. The huge ball bounced off her trunk before it rolled down the embankment, collided with the fallen tree, and shoved the dinobot into the snow. The golem froze as its puppeteer was buried.

With the rear end lightened by five hundred pounds, Cutie's back wheels were able to push her back onto the embankment. She rattled as she rolled among the junk and found a place to hide. Without her rear lights, the riverbank was plunged into darkness.

"Anybody bring a flashlight?" I asked.

"Dan gave us a couple." Oliver handed me one. I aimed it where the dinobot had fallen, swept it back and forth along the bank. I saw its tracks in the snow.

"It went that way!" I pointed with the beam of my flashlight.

The golem woke again and plodded toward Cutie on its mighty piston legs. She headed back toward the fence, slow and wobbly. One of her rear tires had gone flat. The golem caught up easily.

I followed the dinobot's tracks around the piles of junk until they disappeared into a pipe. It was the one with the otters, and something was right in the opening. I hurried over, fell to my knees, and peered in. Sometimes I am not that smart.

I saw a flash of blue light and threw my weight to the

side. The electric bolt seared the collar of my parka. The dinobot emerged from the pipe and leveled its sinister blue eyes at me. I backed away until the ground disappeared: I'd backed right off the ledge. I flailed, found a handhold, and held on. I'd been saved by the otters' makeshift ladder.

The dinobot scuttled over and took aim. In a split second, I calculated my odds of surviving a fifty-foot drop. If I was *lucky*, I would only break every bone in my body. This is what I got for picking a girl over a robot, I thought.

Something heavy, wet, and sharp tore up my back. I felt my coat rip and a dozen daggers pierce my body. A lightning bolt of chestnut brown flew over my head, met the robot dead-on, and knocked it to the ground, then scrambled on to the pipe.

In the distance, the hammering noise stopped. I pulled myself back to the top of the embankment, and Oliver helped me up.

The robot moved, but Oliver gave it a boot stomp, then another, then kicked it off the ledge.

"We were on our way to help you," said Rocky.

"Just three more seconds, we would have been here," said Oliver.

"I know," I told them. "The important thing is, we won." I offered a fist, and they bumped it.

There was a terrific crunch of metal, and the earth shook. We all hit the ground, expecting the sky to fall down around us. There was another, smaller, but still deafening noise, and another. The golem must still be alive. There must be a fifth dinobot controlling it. I groaned. If there was a fifth, there could be a sixth, a seventh, an eighth.

I got up to my knees, saw what was going on, and laughed.

"Come on. Get up," I said.

I helped Rocky up, then Oliver. The noise continued unabated.

Across the junkyard, Cutie had brought down the golem. That was the tremendous crash we'd heard. She was now driving into it, again and again, whacking it from one end, then the other, pushing it toward the ledge. With what must have been her last gasp of life, she sent the monstrosity tumbling down the embankment. It rolled, taking out bushes and trees as it did so, causing a minor avalanche of snow.

"That's the match," said Oliver.

I found the dropped flashlight in the snow, handed it to Rocky, and pointed at the pipe. "This is your chance to see an otter."

She crouched down, peered inside, and made a *squee* sound. "Otter puppies," she said. "They're amazing." I peered in and saw the mother looking back at me, glossy black eyes peering cautiously over a puff of damp muzzle.

"Thanks for saving my life," I whispered to the mama otter.

I didn't do it for you, her face seemed to say.

Surrounding her were five or six kitten-sized bundles of soft brown fuzz, peeping and squeaking as they nursed. They were tiny and helpless and more perfect than anything any of us could make ourselves.

CHAPTER 28

Cutie was barely recognizable: All of her glass was shattered, her roof hammered flush with the hood, the tail dragging on the ground.

"It's amazing she still works," said Oliver. "Or, you know, that she worked until a few minutes ago."

"They knew how to make cars back then," said Rocky.

We traded glances, thinking about all the work Sergei had put into this beautiful car. It wasn't going to be restored again. It was beyond all hope.

"She was a good girl," said Rocky. She reached out and gave the car a single affectionate pat. The grille shifted, collapsing on one side, and some of her innards burst out.

"Oops," said Rocky. "Sorry."

Something fell out of the grille and rolled toward me. I picked it up and put it in my pocket.

We limped home, slowly, on layers of ice and snow. I was glad when we got to First Street and the glow of street lamps. Oliver split off first, mumbling that he would see us at school. Rocky and I trod on.

"I wouldn't have done any of this if I didn't want you to like me," I told Rocky.

"That's a dumb reason to do anything," she said.

"I don't know. Maybe. Probably."

"I already liked you," she said. She took my hand, gave it a squeeze.

I walked her home, then let myself in my house through the back door.

"Is that you?" Mom's voice called from the living room.

"Yeah." So much for sneaking in and going to bed.

She appeared in the doorway and flipped on the light. "Thank God you're all right."

"I'm fine," I said. I took off my jacket and hung it up. "I didn't mean to keep anyone up."

"Well, go to bed. We'll talk in the morning." She gave me a hug. "You're in big trouble," she said.

"All right." I didn't care. At least I was alive.

I waited for Mom to leave, grabbed something from my jacket pocket, and went upstairs. Mom had already gone to bed.

I went into the bathroom and awkwardly sloshed peroxide on my otter-inflicted wounds, then went to my room. Penny crept in a moment later.

"You did it, didn't you?" she whispered.

"Yeah, we did it, and we won."

"I knew it!" she said.

"You know because you saw it happen." I handed her the

camera that had fallen from Cutie's grill. "Better get this cleaned up and back in the box before Dad finds it."

"I will." She took the camera. "I didn't get to see all of it. Dad kept asking me what I was doing on the computer."

"We'll watch it later. Now go to bed." She did, and I changed into jammies and crawled into bed myself. It felt like I'd just fallen asleep when Dad popped into my room. "Glad you could make it home. Don't forget you have to shovel."

He did let me sleep for another couple of hours before I went out to shovel. I was tired and sore, and the snow was wet and heavy. A fine way to treat a hero, I thought. The new ache in my back harmonized nicely with the sting of my scratches. Penny came out to help, scattering rock salt behind me as I shoveled snow and scraped ice.

Mom was waiting when I got inside, a mug of cider in her hands. She handed it to me.

"I think it's time to talk about last night," she said.

Dad was there, too, his face serious but calm. My eyes met his.

"Go ahead," he said. "Tell us what happened."

"I'll show you," I said.

I burned the video to two DVDs, and we watched it as a family on TV: thirty-seven clips of the robot's-eye view of the world. We skipped over Rocky and Oliver finishing their work and fast-forwarded to the battle. It made me a little seasick to see the screen flashing by garbage, steamrolling dinobots, hanging precariously on the ledge as the golem's fists swung overhead.

"Hooray!" Penny shouted when the golem finally went over the edge, as seen by Cutie as she gave it the last big shove.

Mom and Dad watched in stunned silence.

Dad shook his head. He was too dazed to be angry. "You run through all the scenarios in your head," he said. "All the trouble your kids might get into. This one, I didn't expect."

"Me neither," I said.

"How did you even . . . get involved with all this?" Mom asked.

I thought back to when I chose the girl over the robot, but I didn't need to go back that far.

"I guess it was when I took Dad's cameras," I told them.

The news was full of reports about Nomicon—the fence broken down, a decade's worth of junk tossed around, noises audible for miles, all in the middle of a late-season blizzard. Hooligans playing with heavy machinery, some of the reporters speculated. It wasn't clear if they found Cutie—the police didn't give away that much. Dmitri told me in an IM it was fine if they did. Sergei had blasted off the VIN, just in case.

They never came up with any real answers. Eventually, lawyers representing the real estate company that owned the land requested they close the investigation. The request was granted, and the fences went back up. The mystery on Half Street faded from the headlines. Nomicon was going to be forgotten once again.

On the last Saturday in March the Volkovs had a party for Sergei's acquittal. Less than two weeks had passed, but all the snow from the storm had disappeared. It felt like spring. There were even robins flitting about in the naked branches of the trees outside.

The Volkov house was full of people and buzzing with conversations, a mix of English and Russian. I stood in the kitchen, had a piece of crumbly vanilla cake and two cups of orange-scented tea while Malasha talked to a goth girl named Mandy. I was a bit lonely, but all right—there was something warm and comforting about the Volkovs' house. With all the problems Dmitri talked about, the place felt like a home.

"Having fun?" Dmitri asked me.

"Sure. Hey." We slapped hands.

"Thanks for coming," he said. "Rocky and Oliver coming?"

"I don't know. I've been out of commission. Flu."

"Rocky just said 'maybe' on the invite," he said. "Oliver never responded. I thought, you know, the four of us could hang out again."

"Me too," I said. "I'd like that."

"I'm feeling kind of left out these days," he admitted, then laughed nervously. "I guess it's my own fault for blowing off the battle, huh?"

"No, no. That's not it. I've been grounded and haven't seen anybody outside of school, either." I didn't know what else to tell him. The three of us had been through something—an adventure—that he had not. "Anyway, you did the right thing," I reminded him. "Putting your family first. That was responsible. Thoughtful."

"Yeah," he said. "I'm the good one. I know." He gulped some lukewarm tea. "Hey, wait until you see the surprise we have for Sergei," he said. "You might see him cry."

"Ha." It was easier to believe I'd see Sergei *fly*.

Rocky did come, carrying her bike helmet, explaining it was too nice a day not to ride. I made a note to get my own bike tuned up so I could go on rides with her that summer. Oliver came, too, but he doesn't like rooms full of strangers. He preferred to hang out in the TV room with Alexei, watching muted parrots on the plasma screen.

After an hour or so, everybody trickled out to the backyard for the big surprise. A car was under a tarp. Had Dmitri somehow rescued the Mustang? I wondered. Dan Clouts had helped us cart it back to the storage place, but the car was a wreck.

The four of us stood on the back porch and watched: Rocky and me on the lower step, Oliver and Dmitri behind us.

Sergei looked skeptically at the tarp-covered car. "Is this what I think it is?" He yanked the cloth away.

I'd heard the expression "love at first sight," but I didn't know what it meant until I saw Sergei and that ugly green car.

He circled it, reached out, and touched it as tentatively as if it were an untamed horse.

"It is a Superbird," he said. "I didn't completely believe it, but here it is."

I'd forgotten all about the car Dmitri discovered at the junkyard. Sergei inspected it, checking the side panels and the wheels and the bumpers. "It's all here, too. Even the air wing." He ran his hand along the crazy big spoiler. "Do I dare ask about the engine?"

"There's an engine *in it*," said Dmitri. "It's old, but I don't know for sure if it's the original one."

Sergei popped the hood, looked at the engine, and burst into tears.

Dmitri edged over to me. "I told you," he whispered.

"I don't get it," I admitted. "It's kind of an ugly car."

"Beauty is in the eye of the beholder," he reminded me. He leaned in to whisper. "And, uh, restored Superbirds can go for over a million bucks at auction."

One day that summer, just before the Fourth of July, I biked to the University of Minnesota. I remembered the oddly shaped building where Peter Clayton worked, and the way to his office. Oliver assured me he would be there. I caught Peter alone, eating a sandwich, his sleeves rolled up so he wouldn't drip on them.

"Jim!" He put down the sandwich and grabbed some napkins to wipe his hands. "What a surprise. Is Oliver with you?"

"No, it's just me."

"Hmm. OK." He looked at me uneasily. "What can I do for you?"

"I've owed you this for a while," I told him. "You know, for the cameras you pretended to buy? My dad helped me calculate interest. Seven percent." I gave him a check, already written out.

"Knox and Sons," he noted. "So you went into business with your dad?" He set the check on the desk.

"Actually, I went into business for myself," I told him. "But people like to think there's a grown-up behind the scenes, you know?"

"I imagine. So, what do Knox and Sons do?"

"Mow lawns," I said. "Hopefully shovel snow, come winter. I have three workers now, hope to make it five by the end of the summer."

He laughed. "Wow. Very ambitious for a kid your age." I didn't think he believed me. "Well, thanks for coming through on the debt, and I'm glad things are going well for you. But if you, uh, if you were hoping I'd clear your name in the robot competitions, I'm afraid that banned for life means banned for life. Fool me once, you know?"

"Yes, I understand. That's cool. I wasn't going to enter again. My sister is disappointed, but you had to do what you had to do." Penny was devastated when we got the official letter. She'd just started dreaming of next year's competition, and designing Celeste II to compete. I didn't feel good about what I was going to do, but I would do anything for that girl.

"Thanks so much for repaying your debt. Good look with your . . ." Peter waved his hand toward the door. "Your endeavors."

"Thanks. Oh, by the way, Sergei says hi."

"Who?"

"The guy that towed your Audi and hid it until you sold it?"

"Um, I'm sure you're mistaken. My car was *stolen.*"

"I saw your car at Sergei's house. And when I showed him your picture, he said, 'That's the dude.'" I tried unsuccessfully to mimic Sergei's faint accent.

"I have no idea what you're talking about." He fiddled with a pencil on his desk.

"Seems like a long way to go, but you kept asking Oliver's mom to move in, and she kept making excuses not to. Maybe you felt she just needed a little push? Convince her the neighborhood's going to heck, and all that?"

"Now you are touching on personal matters that are really none of your business."

"You're right. But you should know that Sergei nearly got sent to prison for helping you."

"That's not possible," said Peter, his surprise winning out over his caution. "I never filed a police report."

"Maybe you told too many people it was stolen," I said. "The new owner got pulled over and questioned, and told them it was delivered by a Russian guy on a tow truck. They thought it was a big break in a wave of car thefts."

"Well, I never meant to make trouble for the man," he said. "It was a harebrained scheme, done out of love. Tell him I'm sorry."

"We all make mistakes."

Peter sighed. "You know, I suppose a child as young as your sister might have been confused about the rules, and can be granted a second chance. I can't make any promises, but I think if I wrote a letter, she could be cleared for future competitions."

"Thank you. That's really cool of you." I offered him a fist, but he didn't bump it.

I cycled home, glad for the breeze blowing off the river. I took the bike trail north along the Mississippi and turned west down the boulevard to my own home. I'd seen plans to expand the river trail north, right through the leveled ground where Nomicon used to stand. There would be a park there, a place for bikers to pull off and take a break, a playground and wading pool. The neighborhood association was behind it. I've been going to the meetings lately; us local business owners have to get involved. I lobbied for the name "Ted Whaley Memorial Park," but it didn't fly. On the bright side, I got them to write into the charter that the otters would be safe.

I still had six lawns to mow, which was a light day for me. I got my crew and headed across the alley. They all went to work—one mowing, one edging, one raking up loose grass and bagging it. I'd also brought a collapsible chair and my new laptop, sat down to supervise and do a little work on the computer. I barely had it open before Rocky saw me and came out.

"The Knox boys hard at work," she said.

"Yeah," I said. Maybe Knox & Sons was an appropriate name, after all.

I'd created Blade first, recycling a lot of code from robot wars into an electric mower. The Edge came next, and finally Princess Daisy. PD was the raker—I'd made the mistake of letting Penny name her, since she'd helped design it. Dan Clouts had put up the money for parts, but I'd already paid him back. Now that I was out of debt with Peter, too, I could finally start turning a profit.

"What's next?" Rocky asked. "A robot that pulls weeds?"

"Lots of requests for that, but I'm not ready to make it," I admitted. "It'll have to be pretty sophisticated to tell a flower from a weed. Right now I'm working on robots to rake and bag leaves in the fall, and when I'm done with those. . . ."

"Something to shovel snow?" she guessed.

"You read my mind."

"So, do you need to keep supervising, or do you want to come in for a soda?" Rocky asked.

"Hmm. They've had a few solo runs and are reliable. PD is kind of a slacker, but Blade will keep an eye on her." I closed up the laptop. My new robot design would have to wait. I went with the girl.

ACKNOWLEDGMENTS

My sincerest thanks to the following people:

My parents, for giving me a love for books and a thirst for knowledge.

An excellent group of friends and writers I'm lucky to call my group: Jeremy Anderson, Kelly Barnhill, Steve Brezenoff, Jodi Chromey, Karlyn Coleman, and Christopher Lincoln.

Christopher Bongaarts and Julia Vogl, for their expertise on robots.

Tina Wexler, for her enthusiasm and support in all my writerly endeavors.

Allison Wortche, for always finding the heart of a story and making it beat stronger.

Sarah Hokanson, for making this manuscript into a beautiful book; and Tim Jessell for the fabulous cover.

The rest of the team at Knopf Books for Young Readers and Random House Children's Books.

Isaac Asimov, for his seminal robot stories.

Angela and Byron, for filling my life with love (and my slippers with Cheerios).

ABOUT THE AUTHOR

KURTIS SCALETTA is the author of *Mudville,* a *Booklist* Top 10 Sports Book for Youth; *Mamba Point,* which the *New York Times Book Review* called "entertaining and touching"; and *The Tanglewood Terror,* a Kids' Indie Next List Selection and winner of the Minnesota Readers' Choice Award. He lives in Minneapolis with his wife and son. To learn more about him and his books, please visit kurtisscaletta.com.

Welcome to Moundville, where it's been raining for longer than twelve-year-old Roy McGuire has been alive. Most people say the town is cursed—right in the middle of their biggest baseball game against rival town Sinister Bend, black clouds crept across the sky and it started to rain. That was twenty-two years ago . . . and it's still pouring.

Baseball camp is over, and Roy knows he's in for a soggy summer of digging ditches in the mud and wishing he were still playing ball. But when he returns home, Roy finds a foster kid named Sturgis sprawled out on his couch. As if this isn't weird enough, just a few days after Sturgis's arrival, *the rain stops.* No one can explain why it's finally sunny, but as far as Roy's concerned, it's time to play some baseball. It's time to get a Moundville team together—with Roy catching and Sturgis pitching—and finish what was started twenty-two years ago. It's time for a rematch.

When his dad gets a job at the U.S. embassy in Liberia, twelve-year-old Linus knows it's his chance for a fresh start. Instead of his typical anxious self, from now on he'll be cooler and bolder: the new Linus. But as soon as Linus's family arrives, they encounter a black mamba—the deadliest snake in Africa. And before long, Linus is sure the venomous serpents are somehow drawn to him; he can barely go outside without tripping over a mamba.

Then he hears about kasengs—and the belief that some people have a mysterious connection to certain animals. Linus knows he has to get over his fear of his kaseng animal. Soon he's not only keeping a black mamba in his laundry hamper; he's also feeling braver than ever before. Is it his resolution to become the new Linus, or does his sudden confidence have something to do with his scaly friend?

The wilderness abounds with monsters that take many forms, some never imagined by storytellers. . . .

When thirteen-year-old Eric Parrish comes across glowing mushrooms in the woods behind his house, he's sure there's a scientific explanation. But then they begin to encroach on the town, covering the football field and popping up from beneath the floorboards of his house. It doesn't take long for Eric to realize something's seriously wrong.

Then Eric meets Mandy, a runaway girl from the nearby boarding school, who warns him that the fungus could portend the town's doom, leaving it in rubble—just like the village that disappeared in the exact same spot over two hundred years ago. Halloween is approaching, the fungus is spreading, and Eric and Mandy set out to solve a very old mystery and save the town of Tanglewood.